"Olivia!" C‌‌‌‌‌‌‌‌‌
beneath the water for a sign of her.
"Where are you?"

"I'm here, Cal. I'm right here."

He swiveled around. Olivia was in the corner, hiding behind some shelves, almost impossible to see in the dark. Only the whites of her eyes and the glint of a knife were clearly visible.

"Hold on to me," he said, swimming over to her. "Let's get you out of here."

She took his hand and slowly moved from her hiding spot. Her face was etched with fear.

"Where did the gunman go?" she asked. "Is he dead?"

As if the attacker himself decided to answer this question, he suddenly burst through the water close to the stairs, where he was able to easily climb out. With deep and ragged breaths, he clambered up the steps and ran with heavy feet across the floor of the café above. Within a few seconds, all traces of him were gone...

Elisabeth Rees was raised in the Welsh town of Hay-on-Wye, where her father was the parish vicar. She attended Cardiff University and gained a degree in politics. After she met her husband, they moved to the wild rolling hills of Carmarthenshire, and Elisabeth took up writing. She is now a full-time wife, mother and author. Find out more about Elisabeth at elisabethrees.com.

Books by Elisabeth Rees

Love Inspired Suspense

Caught in the Crosshairs
Innocent Target
Safe House Under Fire
Hunted by the Mob
Uncovering Alaskan Secrets
Wyoming Abduction Threat
Submerged Secrets

Navy SEAL Defenders

Lethal Exposure
Foul Play
Covert Cargo
Unraveling the Past
The SEAL's Secret Child

Visit the Author Profile page at LoveInspired.com.

SUBMERGED SECRETS

ELISABETH REES

LOVE INSPIRED SUSPENSE
INSPIRATIONAL ROMANCE

LOVE INSPIRED® SUSPENSE
INSPIRATIONAL ROMANCE

PLEASE RECYCLE
THIS PRODUCT IS RECYCLABLE

Recycling programs
for this product may
not exist in your area.

ISBN-13: 978-1-335-98066-3

Submerged Secrets

Love Inspired
22 Adelaide St. West, 41st Floor
Toronto, Ontario M5H 4E3, Canada
www.LoveInspired.com

Printed in Lithuania

MIX
Paper | Supporting
responsible forestry
FSC® C021394

Be of good courage, and he shall strengthen
your heart, all ye that hope in the Lord.
—*Psalm* 31:24

For my mother.

ONE

Bobbing on the surface of the floodwater was a skull, its pure white sheen almost luminous in the darkness.

Frozen in shock, Olivia Moretti stopped wading and simply stared at it, while waist deep in the cellar of her flooded café in Abbeywood, New Hampshire. She'd only traveled to the café to remove a few items from behind the counter, but a crashing noise from the cellar had forced her to go investigate. She'd then discovered that a wall behind the steel storage racks had collapsed, and she'd ventured into the floodwaters to find out why. That was when she saw the skull on the surface, floating on a piece of ragged tarpaulin that was slowly sinking as water crept onto the edges.

In the gloom, she heard the sound of her quickened breaths combined with the slow trickle of water that was descending the stairs from the flooded café. The Abbey River had burst its banks in the early hours of the morning and caused widespread flooding in the town center. Six inches of water had already seeped under the front door of Moretti's and had been steadily filtering into the cellar ever since.

"It must be an animal skull," Olivia told herself, watching the white cranium disappear into the murky depths. "It can't be human." She blinked fast. "Can it?"

Her gaze traveled to the site of the collapsed wall, which had revealed another wall behind it. She narrowed her eyes to get a better look. The electricity was out, and the cellar windows were not only small but level with the sidewalk, making the entire space gloomy and dim. As she studied the area, the situation became clearer. It looked like somebody had built a false wall a little in front of the original one, leaving a hidden space between the two, and the recent floodwaters had seeped into the cement, causing it to lose strength. Her relief at realizing that this damaged wall had not been structurally important was quickly replaced with fear. What if somebody had used this cavity to hide a body? What if the skull was human after all?

Shaking away the ridiculous notion, she inched her way forward, heading to the folded tarpaulin that was wedged in the hollow space between the two walls, currently above the waterline. She hadn't remembered this blue tarp being in the cellar before now, but it was clearly old, showing plenty of cracks. Reaching out to touch it gingerly, she jumped back when it began to fall forward. Without warning, the edges opened up to reveal a skeleton, minus the skull. She screamed in horror as bones fell onto her. She crossed her arms over her head, stumbling backward and losing her footing. She fell beneath the surface, screaming into the water, feeling the smooth, hard bones brushing her bare arms. She panicked, not knowing which way was up. Her legs somehow got caught in the tarpaulin and it seemed to cling to her like a second skin, holding her down. She couldn't breathe.

Just as she felt herself grow dizzy, a hand gripped tightly onto her shoulder. In a split second, the tarp was unraveled from her legs, and the hand moved from her shoulder to the waistband of her shorts. Then she was yanked upward and placed on her feet in the waist-deep water. She gasped for air.

"Stay calm, Olivia," her rescuer said, holding her shoulders as she wiped the water from her face. "You're okay. Take deep breaths. I was out on the street when I heard you scream. What's going on?"

"There's…a…body," she managed to say, squeezing her eyes shut so she wouldn't catch sight of any more bones. "Under the water."

"A body? You mean a dead body?"

She nodded. "Bones. They fell from the wall."

As the man splashed over to the cavity in the wall, she opened her eyes and noticed his yellow high-visibility jacket with the name Mackenzie written on the hemline. The man who'd saved her was Cal Mackenzie, the Abbeywood fire chief.

She inwardly groaned. Cal was the last person she would've wanted to come to her aid. They weren't exactly the best of friends.

Twenty-five years ago, the Mackenzies opened their own café in Abbeywood and it became a competitor to Moretti's. Although Olivia had been a child at the time, she'd been encouraged by her grandfather to shun their business rivals. Mario Moretti established his successful Italian eatery almost seventy years ago and he'd hated the way Mackenzie's Café flagrantly copied his menu, serving tiramisu, profiteroles and panna cotta alongside other Italian favorites. Cal had worked in his family's café straight out of high school but stepped away several years ago to enter the fire service. Now he apparently wanted to return to the hospitality industry as his own boss, because he'd recently made an offer to purchase a café in Abbeywood to run as a solo project. And that café was Olivia's. That sale would only happen over her dead body.

Olivia shook herself back into the current moment. This wasn't the time to worry about a business sale that absolutely wasn't going to happen. Not when there literally was a dead body in the vicinity and she had no idea who it was.

"Looks like somebody built a false wall here a long time ago," Cal said, shining his flashlight from top to bottom. "If you saw bones fall from it then we have a crime scene on our hands. I'll go call Bear."

Bear was the nickname of the county sheriff, Roger Quaid. With his huge stature and big bushy beard he suited the moniker well.

Cal waded toward Olivia and reached for her hand. "I'll help you up the stairs. You must be freezing."

She declined his offer with a firm shake of her head. "I don't need your help, Cal. I'll be fine."

Even in the darkness, she saw the eye roll. "Seriously, Olivia, are you holding a grudge because I made an offer to buy Moretti's Café?"

"Absolutely."

He sighed. "My offer is a good one." He headed to the staircase. "Let's not allow business to get in the way of a beautiful friendship."

She followed him up the stairs, dripping wet and shivering in her denim cutoffs and T-shirt. She knew he was teasing her with his usual snark, yet she couldn't help but rise to the bait.

"Friendship?" she asked incredulously. "We don't have any friendship at all, let alone a beautiful one."

He stopped and turned when he reached the main café area, where the dark wood paneling and marble countertops harkened back to the 1950s, when her grandfather first established the business.

"Don't you remember senior prom?" he asked with an infuriating smirk. "Behind the drapes?"

She felt her face flush. That had been a moment of madness, which she'd regretted ever since. After humiliating herself at prom by falling awkwardly on the dance floor, Olivia had hidden behind the long drapes in the school gymnasium. Cal had also been hiding there, after his date decided to hook up with the captain of the football team. Both sad and dejected, they'd put aside their differences to commiserate with each other. Before she knew what she was doing, she had kissed him for a full minute. But worse than that, she'd enjoyed it. No matter how much Olivia wanted to hate him, Cal's pale blue eyes, sandy curls and smattering of freckles made her lose herself sometimes. Her attraction to him was a weakness she needed to guard against, because her grandfather had repeatedly warned her to never trust a Mackenzie.

"We were eighteen, Cal," she said. "It was fourteen years ago now, so I think we can go ahead and forget it."

He smiled, revealing a cute dimple on one side. "You can forget it if you want, but I'll keep it right here." He tapped his forehead. "You kissed me, and you liked it."

"Shut up." Why did she always bite when he annoyed her? "I was young and naive."

"Whatever."

He took off his jacket and placed it around her shoulders, rubbing her upper arms firmly to warm her up.

"You should sit in my truck with the heat on," he said, slipping his cell phone out of the chest pocket on his shirt. "I'll take you home as soon as Bear arrives to secure the scene."

"I'll stay here a little while," she said, sitting on the counter. "Maybe one of Bear's deputies can take me home."

Cal shrugged. "Suit yourself."

As he walked through the door and began speaking on his cell phone, Olivia found herself regretting shunning his offer. In the cold, silent darkness, she remembered she was sharing the space with the remains of a potential murder victim.

There had to be a rational explanation for this strange occurrence. There was no way a member of her family was a killer. Perhaps the body and the false wall had been placed there before her grandfather purchased the building.

"It's nothing to worry about," she said to herself. "Just wait and see."

Nevertheless, a sense of unease settled in her gut, telling her she was dead wrong.

Cal placed another blanket around Olivia's shoulders, ignoring the look of disdain she threw his way. He'd guessed she would react angrily to his offer to buy Moretti's Café, but she was determined to dislike him no matter what he did, so he'd made the decision to act in spite of her objections. Besides, it made sense for the Morettis to cut their losses and sell up. Cal heard through the grapevine that Olivia's father, Leonardo, had applied for a bank loan to save the business but had been turned down. Moretti's was in serious financial difficulty.

Although Cal loved his job as fire chief, he missed the hustle and bustle of life in a café. He had a grand plan to combine his business skills with his Christian faith. He felt a strong desire to serve the most vulnerable people in society by feeding them and providing warm spaces to talk or pray. His dream was to set up two or three cafés across the state and use the profits to fund a shelter and church for homeless people in the capital. When he'd heard about Moretti's Café falling into possible bankruptcy, it had felt like a blessing on his plan. If he bought out the café, he could hit the ground running, sparing himself all the new-business hassles of building up a brand, reputation and customer base by taking over an operation that was already well-known and well-liked. *And* he'd be able to save a local institution, keeping the place from having to close its doors after all these years. It seemed like a win-win.

Of course, there was still the question of why the business was in so much trouble in the first place. Moretti's was the most popular café in Abbeywood, always full to the rafters with happy diners. That's why Cal struggled to understand why it was losing money. He suspected the place was being mismanaged by Leonardo, and he'd insist on full disclosure before the purchase went through. But if, as he suspected, it was a question of some bad business decisions that had spiraled out of control, then he believed he'd be able to turn things around.

"You don't need to stay here now the body's been removed, and Bear has everything under control," Olivia said, sitting on the café's marble counter. "It's getting dark outside, so you should go home."

Although Bear was in the cellar with two forensic experts, Cal didn't want to leave Olivia upstairs by herself.

"I think you need somebody with you," he said. "How about I call your dad?"

She shook her head. "He's busy. He's not able to come."

"What about Rosalie?" Rosalie was Olivia's best friend, who'd been working at Moretti's for the past five years.

"I'm fine, Cal," Olivia snapped. "Just go. You've done enough damage already."

He took a step back at her hostile tone. Since childhood,

he and Olivia had shared a tumultuous relationship. They'd been encouraged by Mario to view one another as natural enemies. Cal felt certain that Olivia never told her grandfather about their unexpected kiss back in high school. Mario would've been horrified.

"Listen to me," he said. "Your café is in trouble. If your father doesn't sell to somebody, you'll go bust eventually."

"I'll find a way to plug the holes. This café is my grandfather's legacy, and it should stay in my family."

"I heard that the bank turned down your dad's loan application," he said. "If a bank won't lend money to the business, it's not likely anybody else will."

She jumped from the counter, splashing into the water. Then she glared at him. He ran his gaze up and down her figure. She was wearing frayed denim shorts that showed off her long, slender legs, along with rubber boots that ended at the knee. Beneath the blanket around her shoulders, she wore a raggedy orange T-shirt with a faded purple logo. Olivia was the only woman in Abbeywood who could still look beautiful while dressed in clothes that even Goodwill would probably toss out. She had classic Italian features: olive skin, deep brown eyes, long, curly dark hair and an expressive face. Olivia's face hid nothing. The way she screwed up her nose, pinched her lips or rolled her eyes always revealed her moods. And right at that moment, her expression was telling him to back off.

"Okay," he relented, holding his palms in the air. "I'll give you some time to talk over my offer with your dad and your grandmother."

"Nonna's dementia has gotten bad," she said, referring to her grandmother using the Italian term. "That's why my dad can't get here. She can't be left alone. He has full control of Moretti's now, and he makes the financial decisions."

"Oh." He bowed his head. "I'm sorry. I haven't seen Francesca at church in a while. I should've asked after her."

Cal's heart heaved for Olivia, in spite of their difficulties. Not only had she lost her grandfather six years ago, but her mother, Penny, had died of breast cancer just three years later. Now, on top of those bereavements, her grandmother, Francesca, was afflicted with dementia. Life didn't seem fair.

"I'll pray for you," he said, seeing Bear emerge through the door of the cellar with a cell phone in hand. "Every day."

She gave him a weak smile. The one thing they agreed on was a belief in God's healing grace.

Bear came to stand between them, his face solemn. He was wearing waterproof waders over his sheriff's uniform, and Cal noticed that the waterline on the fabric indicated rising flood levels. He should probably conduct another assessment of the river before too long.

"I just got a call from the coroner," Bear said. "There's a skull fracture on the victim that indicates the cause of death was blunt force trauma. This has all the hallmarks of a murder."

This came as no surprise to Cal. Why would somebody go to such lengths to conceal a body unless they'd committed a crime?

"That's not all," Bear continued. "The coroner noticed the victim had an extra tooth that partly extended into her nasal cavity. Because the condition is so rare, he contacted a dentist here in Abbeywood, to see if he could help with identification. The dentist remembered treating a woman with the same condition thirty years ago, so he pulled her dental records. There was a one hundred percent match to the victim. Her name is Sadie Billingham. Her husband and stepson have been informed of the discovery of her body."

"I'll pray for her family. But…do you really think she was murdered?" Olivia asked, as if she'd been hoping Bear would have a much simpler explanation.

"That's my theory right now. Sadie was forty years old when she disappeared from Abbeywood thirty years ago. Her husband, Randy, thought she'd moved to New York. She left him a Dear John letter that he said looked convincing. I was a deputy back then, and I remember being a little surprised that Sadie left her stepson so easily, even though he was an adult by that point. But I figured she just wanted to get away from here, no matter the personal cost. She'd been having a long-term affair with a local married man, but he broke it off and she was pretty cut-up about it. Everybody assumed she wanted to start afresh in the city."

"But she didn't start afresh, did she?" Olivia said. "She ended up buried in the cellar of Moretti's Café. How did that happen?"

Bear cleared his throat nervously, betraying the seriousness of the news he was about to impart.

"I'm sorry to break it to you, but I suspect your grandfather killed Sadie and hid her body in the cellar all those years ago."

"What?" The way Olivia let out a sudden laugh revealed how impossible she found the idea. "That's the most ludicrous thing I ever heard."

"Your grandfather was the married man having a long-term affair with Sadie," Bear said. "The only person who didn't know about it was your grandmother."

"Nonno would never kill anybody." Olivia was pacing back and forth, kicking up the water with her rubber boots. "You knew him, Bear. He was a good man."

"Was he?" the sheriff asked with a raise of his eyebrow. "Plenty of folks in Abbeywood might disagree."

"That's not fair. He was grouchy, but that doesn't make him a killer. You can't pin the blame on him without investigating."

"Given the state of the body, there isn't much physical evidence to work with," Bear said. "I'll make some enquiries, but Mario is currently my only suspect in the case."

"I'll find out what happened to Sadie," she said firmly. "I'll investigate this crime myself."

"You're not qualified to investigate a crime," Cal interjected. "Digging into the past when you don't know what you're looking for risks hurting people. Let Bear handle it."

She turned on him. "Why would I take advice from a man who's trying to ruin my life? Stop pretending to care about me, Cal, because I know it's just a tactic to win me over. I'll never support your offer to buy the café, no matter how nice you pretend to be."

These comments wounded him. He and Olivia had a history fraught with tension, but he would never deliberately seek to hurt her.

She stalked toward the door, pulling her car keys from her pocket. "I need some time to think."

Cal knew better than to go after her. "Drive slowly," he called out. "And go straight home. We'll secure the place for the night."

When she'd gone, Bear folded his arms and turned to Cal with a weary sigh.

"That poor girl has been through so much already," he said. "I wish I could make everything better for her."

"Me too," Cal agreed. "Me too."

A few hours later, Olivia sat in the darkness of the café with tears streaming down her face. She was holding a photograph of her grandfather, which normally had pride of place on the wall above the coffee machine. In the black-and-white picture, a young Mario smiled broadly, wearing a long white apron while standing beneath the striped awning of the café. Both windows at either side of the entrance were emblazoned with gold lettering, spelling out MORETTI'S.

There was no way she would believe her grandfather was a killer. Somebody was out to get him—and it could be anybody. Although Mario had been a big character in the community, he had not been universally liked. With a hot temper and an occasionally barbed tongue, he seemed to get into a bitter feud with someone new almost every day. Diners had overlooked his flaws to enjoy his superior baking skills and authentic Italian flair, and most people shrugged off his more over-the-top behavior, but there were those who took the grudges to heart. Perhaps an old adversary had planted the body there to frame him. It was a weak theory, but it was all she could come up with.

Olivia had made a number of phone calls to several people that evening, trying to track down somebody who might be able to shed light on the matter. She knew nothing about Sadie's life in Abbeywood, so she'd selected older members of the community at random, hoping they might remember her. But nobody wanted to talk. All Olivia had done was irritate people, just as Cal had predicted. She hated proving him right. She didn't want him to be right about anything, especially the likelihood of Moretti's entering bankruptcy. The café was still thriving and busy, so Olivia was puzzled about their monetary difficulties. They should be booming. Her father kept strict control of the books and wouldn't let Olivia take over, which frustrated her. She'd have to try once more to persuade him to hand over financial control to her. After all, she managed the café on a daily basis, while her father cared for her grandmother.

Her cell buzzed in her hand and her best friend's name flashed on the display. Olivia and Rosalie went back a long way, all the way to kindergarten. Olivia had jumped at the chance to employ Rosalie in the café when her friend had been looking for work five years ago. They not only had a great friendship but a successful working partnership too. Olivia undertook most of the food preparation, and Rosalie charmed the customers while serving. Two other part-time employees also acted as waiting staff, completing their small but perfect team of four.

"Hi," Olivia said on answering the call. "I'm guessing you heard the bad news through the grapevine."

"You know how effective the Abbeywood grapevine is," Rosalie replied. "Your dad called me. He said you're not picking up his calls, and he's worried about you. I guess you're at the café."

A twinge of remorse pricked Olivia's conscience. There was no way her dad could leave her grandmother alone, so she knew he was stuck at the house. But she hadn't felt ready to answer his calls. Instead, she'd sent him a message saying she wanted to get things straight in her head before having a conversation.

"Yeah, I'm at the café, but I'm going home right now." She slid from her seated position and placed Mario's photo back on the wall. "I need to leave before Cal Mackenzie discovers I'm here. He thinks I went home already."

"Who cares what Conceited Cal thinks?" her friend said with a laugh. "But you should go home anyway."

Olivia laughed along. She and Rosalie had come up with the name Conceited Cal in seventh grade. Rosalie had been Olivia's constant ally in her rivalry with Cal and was the only person Olivia had told about their stolen kiss behind the drapes.

"Thanks for prompting me to get out of here," Olivia said. "I'll call you tomorrow. We'll talk then."

"Sure. Drive safe."

Olivia hung up the phone and picked up her purse. Then she wiped her tear-streaked face and ran her hands through her frizzed-up hair. She must look a mess, but what did it matter? There was nobody in her life to impress.

"Snap out of your funk," she said to herself as she opened the door. "You're wallowing in…"

She froze midsentence. The long barrel of a gun greeted her on the other side of the door. And it was pointed directly at her face. Instinct quickly kicked in, and she lashed out with her hand, knocking the barrel away with a terrified scream. The man holding the gun was wearing a dark green oilskin jacket with the hood pulled up over his forehead. The lower part of his face was hidden by a scarf tied across his mouth. He clearly hadn't been expecting her rapid reaction time, and the trigger of the gun was knocked from his finger. He fumbled with the bulky weapon as she jumped back into the café and attempted to shut the door. But the man placed his foot between the door and the frame beneath the waterline. She screamed and repeatedly pushed against the obstruction while his hand reached through the gap to try to grab her.

The man managed to get ahold of her purse strap on her shoulder and he used it to yank her toward him. She banged her head on the door and cried out in pain. Her attacker attempted the same maneuver once more, gripping the purse strap tight as she pushed with all her might against the door. Shaking her shoulder, she let the strap slide down her arm until the purse dropped into the water, taking her cell phone with it. Olivia felt her attacker's foot shift momentarily from its position, and she used the opportunity to shove the door closed, before securing it with the thumb turn lock.

Then she turned and ran to the counter, opening the drawers to rifle through, pulling out all kinds of utensils and cutlery. In the background, the door was being kicked repeatedly as her assailant tried to gain access. Just as she heard the door frame splinter, she found what she'd been looking for: a six-inch steel-bladed knife. She slid it out of its protective cover and held the knife at her side with a shaking hand. There were no downstairs windows she could squeeze through and no chance of escape. The café's back door had been warped by the floodwater and was stuck fast. She was trapped.

Running through the possibilities of survival, she surmised that the cellar would provide her with the best hiding spot. It was dark, flooded and would be uninviting to a burglar. This man was probably a looter, taking advantage of the fact that the flood had left so many buildings unattended. If he was looking for cash or valuables, he'd find neither in the café. He'd be unlikely to venture into a flooded basement. He'd simply move onto the next property.

With a pounding chest, she slipped through the cellar door and closed it behind her. The small space was enveloped in darkness, and she heard the water gently lapping against the walls. She waited for her eyes to adjust to the dimness. Thankfully, the clouds had momentarily passed, and a bright moon shone outside, providing a pale and watery light. The tiny cellar windows only allowed a little moonlight through, but given how well she knew the space, it was just enough to guide her. As she descended the stairs, she remembered that this area was a burial ground and a crime scene. She contemplated finding somewhere else to hide but she now had no choice. Her attacker was already inside the café, his heavy footsteps reverberating overhead. Hence, she ventured into the darkness, removing her yellow raincoat and laying it on the stairs. Discarding the bright jacket would make it more difficult to spot her hiding in the water.

Taking a deep breath, she plunged into the murky water, holding on to the brickwork at the edges to prevent her falling beneath the surface. The cellar was no longer flooded only to waist height. The waterline had vastly increased, and Olivia wasn't able to touch the floor with her feet. Within a couple hours, the cellar would likely be entirely submerged. The closed windows provided some protection, but the water was slowly seeping through the frames.

Shivering with cold and fear, Olivia swam to the steel racks where the jars of sauces and anchovies were usually stored. All the food items had been moved to a refrigerated unit on the hillside. She held on to the metal frame and swam behind it, pushing her way into the corner, right next to the false wall where Sadie Billingham had gone unnoticed by everyone but her killer for thirty years.

Above her head, the cellar door creaked open and heavy boots seemed to hesitate on the top step. She held her breath. Someone was coming. Peeking through the racking and focusing on the window, she saw car tires grind to a halt at the curb. She could just make out the shape of the wheels through the water. Then a pair of black boots planted themselves on the sidewalk and made their way to the door of the café. There was only one person who would be checking on the floodwaters at this time of night. It had to be the Abbeywood fire chief.

"Please, Cal," she whispered in the dark, uttering words she never thought she'd hear herself say. "Come find me."

The heavy boots on the stairs began to make their way downward until they reached the waterline. There, her attacker hesitated once again, obviously not eager to take the plunge. She saw the outline of his silhouette as he picked up her raincoat from the stairs and threw it into the water. Her assumption regarding his intentions had clearly been wrong. If he'd only been after valuables, he'd have left by now. He wasn't a burglar. He was targeting her. And he still held the gun by his side.

Keeping her breath as silent as she could, she retreated into the shadows, clutching her knife and waited to see what he would do next.

Cal approached the entrance of Moretti's with caution. The police tape that had been secured across the entrance was now floating in the water. He wouldn't be surprised if Olivia had returned to the café once the police left, but she wouldn't have left the door wide open. Perhaps looters were on the prowl. It was a common problem in flooded towns. In one hand, he firmly gripped a flashlight and in the other, he held the gun he always stored in his glove box for personal protection. As he entered the café, he noticed Olivia's purse in the water, its contents scattered. That's when he also noticed the splintered door frame from where the door had been forced open, and he knew something bad had happened. Pocketing his flashlight, he unclipped his radio and tuned it to the emergency channel to call the sheriff's office.

"Calling all Abbeywood law enforcement patrols. This is Fire Chief Caleb Mackenzie. There's been a break-in at Moretti's Café at 121 Main Street. I'm on the scene. A thirty-two-year-old female by the name of Olivia Moretti is believed to be inside and is potentially in danger. Backup requested."

Edging his way into the café, a noise caught his attention. It sounded like movement down below. Moving quickly to the back of the café, he saw the cellar door was ajar. Lifting his flashlight, he kicked the door wide open, aimed the beam down the stairs and pointed his weapon. On the step just above the waterline was a hooded and masked man with a shotgun at his hip. Spooked by the intense beam of light, the man swiveled around and lost his footing. He fell backward into the water and began thrashing his arms and legs.

Cal pocketed his gun and immediately descended the stairs to launch himself into the flooded basement and grapple with the man. He couldn't see much in the blackness of the water and was unable to tell the difference between an arm and a leg while they both twisted and turned. Cal was not only fighting to apprehend the suspect but also struggling to keep himself afloat. His concerns about Olivia added to his anxiety. He had no clue where she was. Her yellow raincoat floated ominously on the water's surface. Was she safe?

"Stop resisting," he ordered the man. "I won't hurt you if you comply."

But compliance was clearly the last thing on this guy's mind. He lashed out with his fists, bobbing above and below the water with the movement. Cal felt himself being dragged down too, as the flailing man grabbed hold of anything within his grasp. Cal kicked out and pushed to the surface to take a deep breath of air. Then he waited for the man to reemerge. Yet the water remained flat and still. He had apparently sunk.

"Olivia!" he yelled, frantically feeling beneath the water for a sign of her. "Where are you?"

"I'm here, Cal. I'm right here."

He swiveled around. Olivia was in the corner, hiding behind some shelves, almost impossible to see in the dark. Only the whites of her eyes and the glint of a knife in her hand were clearly visible.

"Hold on to me," he said, swimming over to her. "Let's get you out of here."

She took his hand and slowly moved from her hiding spot. Her face was etched with fear.

"Where did the gunman go?" she asked. "Is he dead?"

As if the attacker himself had decided to answer this question, he suddenly burst through the water close to the stairs, where he was able to easily climb out. With deep and ragged breaths, he clambered up the steps and ran across the floor of the café above. Within a few seconds, all traces of him were gone.

Cal pulled Olivia through the flooded cellar as quickly as he could. He didn't know how long she had been in the bitterly cold water and was concerned about the onset of hypothermia. She needed to get checked out at the hospital. As he dragged her from the water, her legs gave way beneath her. He took the knife from her hand and laid it on the stair. Then he scooped her into his arms and carried her up the remaining stairs. When they entered the café, Olivia saw the scrawled words on the wall before he did. She gasped and pointed at the whiteboard above the counter. Someone had left a message in huge, black capitals.

LET SADIE REST IN PEACE.

"It's a warning," she said weakly, as Cal checked the street both ways before carrying her to his truck. "Someone wants me to back off."

He said nothing. Bear told him that Sadie had conducted many extramarital affairs in the town, and plenty of those men would want their relationships to remain private, even after all these years. Cal had suspected Olivia would upset one of those men by digging into the past. And now she'd gone and poked a hornets' nest. He'd need to keep a close eye on her to make sure she didn't get badly stung.

TWO

Olivia opened the oven and took out a batch of panettone. A wonderful aroma of candied fruit and raisins filled the kitchen, and she wafted the steam from the sweet breads with her hand. Baking was her way of feeling close to her grandfather. Mario had taught her how to bake everything from amaretti to zonclada, and she'd become an expert at her craft. She made most of the desserts and pastries at Moretti's, turning out multiple batches a day to keep up with demand. Her skills as a pastry chef were legendary in Abbeywood.

Tearing off a piece of hot bread, she put it on a plate and padded into the living room in her fluffy socks, which she wore with gray flannel sweats. There, she sat on the couch next to her grandmother as the rain pelted against the windowpane. She intended on taking things easy. After dragging her from the floodwaters the previous night, Cal had taken her to the hospital, where she'd been treated for mild hypothermia and told to rest at home. Now she was waiting to hear from Bear about whether he had any leads on the man who'd attacked her.

"Would you like some panettone, Nonna?" she asked her grandmother. "It's fresh from the oven."

The elderly woman's white hair had been combed, and her

matching slacks and sweater were neatly pressed. Francesca was a woman who'd always liked to dress in well-tailored clothes, so Olivia and her father ensured she continued to look immaculate, even while she was unable to take care of herself.

Francesca smiled. "No thank you, Penny."

Olivia hid a flinch. While she knew it wasn't done in malice, it still hurt when her grandmother didn't recognize her. And it always stung to think of her mother, who wasn't with them anymore. "My name is Olivia, Nonna. I'm your granddaughter. Penny was my mom, and she died three years ago."

Francesca rubbed the papery skin on her forehead with thumb and forefinger. "Ah, yes. I forget."

"I do too," Olivia said. "I sometimes wake up and forget Mom's gone. I miss her."

Her grandmother smiled and returned to staring vacantly into the flames of the fire. Francesca's face was lined from years of hard work. After marrying Mario at the age of twenty, they both immigrated to the US and created a home away from home in Moretti's Café. Francesca had rolled up her sleeves and built the business in partnership with her husband. Even after their son, Leonardo, came along, she continued to undertake the business admin at home while raising him. Now, at the age of eighty-nine, her precious memories were being gradually lost to dementia. It was such a cruel disease.

At that moment, Olivia's father entered the living room, closely followed by Bear and Cal, who were both wearing their respective uniforms. She jumped up and placed her steaming panettone on the table. She hoped the two men would be bringing positive news.

"It smells divine in the house," Bear said, lifting his nose. "You're always baking something amazing, Olivia."

"It's panettone," Leonardo said. "One of Olivia's specialties. There's a whole batch in the kitchen if you're hungry."

"How are you feeling?" Cal asked. "You gave me quite a scare on the way to the hospital last night. I've never seen you look so pale before."

Olivia twisted her index finger in her palm awkwardly. She hated being in Cal's debt. She didn't want to need anything from him, least of all his protection. But she *had* needed it the previous night, and he'd come to her rescue. She appreciated what he'd done. But if he thought that made them friends now, he was about to be disappointed.

"I'm doing fine," she said politely. "Thank you for what you did."

"Is that all he gets?" her father exclaimed, shaking Cal's hand vigorously. "I think we can offer him more than a meek thank-you. He saved your life."

"And I'm really grateful," she said. "I'm sure Cal knows it."

Leonardo walked to the dark wood dresser in the corner, where the family stored all kinds of packaged Italian treats. Francesca and Mario had both loved traditional Italian cookies. Olivia baked them often, but Leonardo also bought a wide selection for Francesca to enjoy whenever she wanted. Leonardo rooted around in the cabinet, his bald head bobbing up and down as he searched. Finally, he stood up, holding a cellophane-wrapped batch of Nocciolini di Canzo.

Handing the packet to Cal, he said, "These are sweet and crumbly cookies from Northern Italy. A small token of our thanks for what you did."

"I was just doing my job, Mr. Moretti," Cal said, taking the packet. "But I appreciate the gift."

"You see, Dad?" Olivia said, slightly irritated by her father fawning over the man who was trying to steal their café. "He was doing his job. He doesn't want a reward."

Her father shot her a look of displeasure. "I know you're unhappy about Cal's offer to purchase Moretti's, but I raised you to be respectful to everyone, even business rivals."

"He's more than a business rival, though," she said. "He's a business vulture, circling the skies while we're wounded."

"Olivia!" Leonardo said sharply. "This is not the time or place to air your grievances."

She dropped her gaze to the floor, realizing she'd gone too far. Describing Cal as a vulture was dehumanizing.

"You're right. I'm sorry."

Cal smiled at her. "It's okay. You've called me far worse names in the past, right?"

She shot him a glare. It felt like he was teasing her again. Throughout high school, Cal had teased her mercilessly, and she'd always risen to his provocations. Well, not anymore. She clamped her mouth shut and said nothing.

It was Francesca who broke the silence, as she let out a cry of joy when spotting the packet in Cal's hands.

"Ah!" she said. "Nocciolini di Canzo. My favorite."

"Come on, Mom," Leonardo said, helping the old lady from the chair. "We'll go get you some lunch while Olivia talks with Cal and Bear."

The men settled themselves on the couch vacated by Francesca and Olivia sat in the armchair, tucking her feet beneath her. Cal placed his cookies on the small table beside him.

"So," she began. "Do you have any idea who attacked me last night?"

"Firstly," Bear said firmly, "nobody was permitted to enter Moretti's last night. That's why we secured tape across the door."

She put her palms in the air. "Yeah, yeah, I know. I guess I owe another apology."

"Olivia was dealing with some shocking news yesterday," Cal interjected, surprising her by coming to her defense. "It's not surprising that she wanted to be in the place where she felt close to her grandfather, right?"

Olivia stared at him. How did Cal know that? She suddenly felt exposed and emotionally vulnerable. He wasn't meant to see her innermost thoughts.

"Actually, I went there to get some belongings I'd left behind," she lied. "And that's when the armed man broke through the door."

"My officers recovered a twelve-gauge shotgun from the water in the cellar," Bear said. "It's a standard weapon that a lot of people keep at home, especially hunters. There are no prints on it, and it's unregistered. There's no way of tracing the owner, so we have no leads at the present time."

"What about the message on the mirror?" she said. "It's got to be a warning. The man who murdered Sadie is trying to scare me into backing off."

Cal and Bear exchanged a loaded glance, and she knew what they were thinking. They'd already pinned the crime on her grandfather.

"My theory makes sense," she argued. "I made a lot of calls last night, so the real killer knows I'm digging for the truth."

"All you did by making those phone calls was upset a whole bunch of people," Bear said. "Sadie's relationships with certain men in the town were complicated, and you're shining a light in places that some people don't want disturbed. I'm guessing your attacker is one of them. You should let Sadie rest in peace."

Olivia stood up and pointed at the window. "How can she rest in peace when her killer is still out there?"

Bear and Cal fell silent, neither one willing to say the words they knew she didn't want to hear.

"My grandfather didn't kill her," she said.

"You don't want it to be true, Olivia," Cal said gently. "That doesn't mean Mario is innocent."

She sighed and sank back into her chair, placing her head in her hands.

"But why would someone other than the killer go to such lengths to stop me investigating the crime?" she asked. "If you're so sure Mario is guilty, it can't do any harm for me to look for more evidence, right?" She raised her head. "Even if my grandfather *is* the murderer, Sadie deserves an investigation."

Bear leaned forward and looked her in the eye. "I'll investigate Sadie's murder, just like I'll investigate the attack on you. This is *my* job, not yours. I have to tread very carefully when asking questions. Sadie was well-known in Abbeywood for having affairs with married men. By dragging up the past, you'll expose her secrets and stir up gossip. Her husband, Randy, doesn't want that to happen. His son, Bobby, lives with him, and Randy wants to protect Bobby from hearing bad things about his stepmother."

Olivia vaguely knew Bobby Billingham. At fifty-one years of age, he still lived with his father. Bobby wasn't Sadie's biological son, but she'd raised him after his birth mom abandoned him when he was just a few months old. Some people in the town cruelly said that Randy only married Sadie because he wanted a woman to cook, clean and take care of his son. Their marriage had reportedly been unhappy, and Sadie never had a child of her own. Olivia had been able to learn that much from her phone calls the night before. The events might be long in the past, but there were still people around from back then who remembered all the gossip.

"Maybe Randy was the man who attacked me in the café," Olivia suggested. "That's why he wants to shut down my questions."

"I'm not sure of Randy's exact age," Bear said skeptically. "But he must be in his seventies. He's a little too old to be chasing women into flooded cellars."

Olivia often saw Randy pass by the café. He took care of himself and was in better shape than many men half his age.

"He's super fit," she said. "He still jogs regularly. He might be trying to stop me finding out he killed his wife." She looked between Bear and Cal as the idea took root. "You should look into that possibility."

"Did Randy also hide his wife's body behind a false wall in your grandfather's café?" Bear asked with a note of sarcasm.

Olivia dropped her head. This was the one major flaw in her argument. She had to admit that the burial location appeared to be the strongest piece of evidence. Who else besides her grandfather could've placed Sadie's body in the cellar? It was part of the riddle she couldn't solve.

"Somebody is trying to warn you off, but they went too far," Bear said. "I'm worried for you, Olivia, and I currently have no leads to help me find who might want to harm you. If you feel threatened in any way again, call 911, but to keep things from getting worse, you should let sleeping dogs lie. It's for your own good."

She said nothing. Bear, sensing her somber mood, stood up.

"I think Olivia needs some time alone," he said, turning to Cal. "Perhaps you could check on her later."

This was exactly what she didn't want. Cal's creeping presence into her life was maddening.

"I don't need Cal to check on me," she said hotly. "I'll be just fine. Rosalie said she'd drop by this afternoon." She fixed Cal with a stare. "She's worried she might be out of a job if the café is sold."

This was a little white lie. Rosalie was a woman of strong faith, who maintained a positive attitude about almost everything, even the prospect of finding a new job. But Olivia wanted to remind Cal about the staff at Moretti's, who relied on their paychecks.

"Nobody will be forced out of their job if I become the new owner," Cal said. "You already have a good team there. There's four of you, right? Including you."

She folded her arms. "That's right, but I don't think my team will want to work for a Mackenzie."

"Let's wait and see, shall we?" He placed a plastic bag by her feet. "I brought the purse you dropped in the water last night. Everything is dried out and your cell phone seems fine, so please carry it with you wherever you go."

"Thank you," she said tersely, lifting the bag, which emitted a musty smell of floodwater.

"The flood levels are still rising so stay home with your family until it's safe to go out."

She looked up at him and threw him her best fake smile. "Sure."

"I mean it, Olivia."

"I understand."

Cal sighed, either with frustration or resignation. She wasn't sure. But he was aware of the fact she wasn't going to fall in line with everything he said. If he wanted to buy her café, he should know she'd fight him all the way.

* * *

Cal anxiously surveyed the damaged riverbank at North Bridge, where the force of the water had washed away chunks of soil and stone. Only one small section of the bank was now preventing the water from surging over the top and onto a bridge that connected two parts of the town of Abbeywood. There was only one thing for it—he'd have to close the bridge.

Returning to his truck, he took out two "BRIDGE CLOSED" signs and cabled-tied them high up on either end of the steel girders, where they'd be visible to motorists. Thankfully, most residents were heeding the warnings of the fire department, and the streets were empty.

Cal sat in the driver's seat of his truck and shook his head like a dog after a bath. Droplets splashed onto the dash and upholstery, but it didn't matter. He couldn't keep much of anything dry and had gotten used to being permanently damp. He was also working from dawn until dusk, spending very little time at his apartment, which was situated in a complex close to the Moretti family home. When purchasing it a couple of years ago, he'd been curious to see how Olivia would react if she ran into him in the neighborhood. Her reactions were predictable. She crossed to the other side of the street if she saw him out jogging, and if she was in her front yard when he drove past her house, she pretended not to notice him. He thought it was funny, and he often waved or called out a greeting, causing her to scowl at him. He'd been teasing her this way ever since he could remember, and it was probably time for him to cut it out. Yet as juvenile as it was, he enjoyed it too much to stop.

Olivia's resentment of the Mackenzies was a trait learned from her grandfather. After the rival café opened up twenty-five years ago, Mario Moretti had persistently refused to talk to any member of the Mackenzie family, including Cal or his parents. Mario had been a small but terrifying man with jet-black hair and a bushy mustache, both of which steadily turned white over the years. As a child, Cal feared the stern-faced Italian, but as he grew into a man, he realized that Mario was simply afraid of a little competition. As it turned out, Abbeywood was easily able to sustain two cafés anyway. Both places were busy, but Moretti's had something Mackenzie's didn't: almost seventy years of history. The beautiful antique interior of Moretti's Café had been preserved for people to enjoy, and numerous photographs on the walls documented the passing of the decades. Diners traveled far and wide to experience the old Italian feel, not to mention the wonderful Mediterranean food. Moretti's financial woes could only be the result of poor management, because it sure had a huge, loyal clientele. Cal would hate to see it close its doors. It was part of the fabric of Abbeywood.

Cal knew Olivia wouldn't support his offer to purchase the place, but Leonardo had requested some time to run the deal past his lawyer. If the sale went ahead, Cal planned on expanding into the state capital, Concord. The café's brand was strong, and there was a definite opportunity for growth. Purchasing an established institution like Moretti's would take a lot of the risk out of setting up his own venture. Cal's parents weren't interested in expanding Mackenzie's. They were happy with the status quo. Hence, buying Moretti's was the best option in realizing his dream. In the right hands, the café could become a popular chain. Cal could then retire from the fire department and do what he loved most—bringing people together in the heart of a community with good food and coffee.

Funneling some of the profits from the business into a

charitable venture was a no-brainer for him. His idea of opening a homeless shelter had first formed two years ago when he'd started volunteering at a soup kitchen in Concord. That was when he'd learned homelessness was on a steep rise in New Hampshire, and he'd been deeply affected by the misery he'd witnessed on the streets. He began to feel God calling him away from the fire department and onto a new path, where he could serve those who needed him. He hadn't quite worked out the finer details yet, but acquiring Moretti's would set him in the right direction. He'd saved a sizable deposit, and the bank had already approved him for a business loan, so he was good to go.

Upsetting Olivia in the buyout process was unavoidable, but he was willing to take it on the chin. He'd happily retain her on the staff if she was content to continue. Her baking skills were second to none, and he'd struggle to find anybody as creative as she was in the kitchen. He shook his head and chuckled. How naive was he to think Olivia Moretti would work for a Mackenzie? She'd spent their high school years calling him names. Until senior prom, that was. The smile grew wider on his face. That kiss had been the best of his life, one which had taken him totally by surprise. He knew it had been a one-off thing. They'd both been at a low point at the time, and they'd momentarily forgotten their feud. The following day, Olivia had reverted to type. But he'd never forgotten it.

He pulled his cell from his pocket as it began to buzz. Leonardo's name flashed on the display.

"Hi, Mr. Moretti," he said on answering the call. "Is everything all right?"

"Olivia's gone out, and I'm worried about her being caught up in the floods," Leonardo replied. "I wondered if you'd be willing to help locate her. I know you're out patrolling, so you might see her on the road. She told me she was turning in for an early night, but when I went into the garage, I saw her car was gone. She won't stop investigating the Sadie Billingham murder. Nothing I say seems to make a difference."

Cal sighed. He'd been expecting Olivia to do something like this.

"Did you call her?" he asked.

"Yeah, but she didn't pick up."

"I'll take a drive around to see if I can find her. The floodwaters are very unpredictable right now, and she might not be aware of which roads to avoid, especially after dark." Cal checked his watch: night would fall in around two hours. "Where do you think she might've gone?"

"Probably over to Randy Billingham's house. She seems to think he knows more than he's admitting." Leonardo clicked his tongue. "I just wish she'd listen to me and stop all this nonsense. But she's always been stubborn."

Cal steeled himself to ask a question that had been on his mind ever since the discovery of the body in the cellar.

"Can I ask you something, Mr. Moretti?"

"Sure," the older man replied. "And please, call me Leonardo."

"Do *you* think your father murdered Sadie?"

There was a slight pause and a quick intake of breath before the answer came.

"Yes," Leonardo said emphatically. "Yes, I do."

Cal didn't remember Sadie at all. He'd been only three years old when she'd vanished, so he knew very little about what had happened. Leonardo was in his sixties. He would surely know a lot more.

"Did you suspect your father of foul play at the time of the murder?" Cal asked. "And did you know about his affair?"

"I found out about my father's relationship with Sadie shortly after Olivia was born. I overheard a couple of ladies in the grocery store gossiping about it, and I was horrified. I confronted my dad, and he admitted it immediately. He promised to end the affair, but I didn't believe him. He was a difficult man, and he could be very selfish at times. Eventually, Sadie skipped town—or so we thought—and the problem went away." He laughed scornfully. "I was actually pleased she'd left Abbeywood. I never imagined she'd been murdered. I didn't suspect my father of doing anything wrong at the time, but she was found in his café. The evidence speaks for itself."

"Didn't you notice the false wall in the cellar? You worked at the café for a while, right? You knew the place well."

"Those racks in the basement are huge and always covered with jars. You can't usually see the wall behind, so I wouldn't have noticed if it looked different. I guess the floor space shrunk a little, but who pays attention to a thing like that? Besides, I was trying to protect my mom back then, making sure she didn't hear any gossip in town about dad's affair. I was kind of preoccupied."

"Okay." Cal started up his truck. "Thanks for the information. I'll get on the road to try to locate Olivia. When I find her, I'll call you right away. Try not to worry. I'm sure she's fine."

"I appreciate your help, Cal." Leonardo paused. "I'm sorry about the animosity between our families over the years. My father was incredibly competitive, so when your family established their café, he didn't deal with the rivalry very well. And he passed along his hostile attitude to Olivia. Since his passing, I've built a bridge with your folks, but Olivia is resistant."

"It doesn't help that I've made an offer to purchase Moretti's," Cal said. "She thinks I'm a vulture. I hope you don't feel the same way."

"Absolutely not. I've been looking over your offer with my lawyer and I'll have an answer for you soon. He says the deal is good."

Cal was pleased to hear this.

"I'll be in touch," he said. "Hang tight."

He ended the call, clipped the cell to his dashboard and pulled away from the curbside. This part of town had escaped the flooding so far, but water had collected in large puddles at the sides of the road. These puddles were easy to spot in daylight but at night, they'd become almost invisible. And hitting a large body of water at speed could easily cause a fatal accident.

With Olivia's safety on his mind, he activated the voice control on his cell and instructed it to call her number. Within seconds, the ringtone resounded in the truck. He let it ring until he heard her voicemail message. Then he hung up. He didn't bother trying again because he knew she wouldn't answer. After all, he was enemy number one.

Olivia rapped on the door of Randy Billingham's home three times. He lived in a big house on a complex called Redwood Estates on the outskirts of town. Although she saw him on occasion, they'd never spoken to each other until she telephoned him after Sadie's body had been discovered in the café. Due to his hostile reaction on the phone, she hadn't been expecting a welcoming smile to greet her. And she'd been right.

"What do *you* want?" Randy asked on opening the door. "I thought I told you to leave me alone."

Randy had a thin physique and weatherworn skin. She

guessed he was retired now but might've worked outside during his life. Nobody seemed to know Randy's profession, and he was something of an enigma.

"I understand you don't want to talk to me, but I'll only take a moment of your time." She held up a hand to implore him to keep the door open and not slam it in her face. "You're the best person who can help me find out who killed your wife."

"Mario Moretti killed my wife," he said, enunciating every word as if Olivia was five years old. "You're the only person in Abbeywood who refuses to believe it."

"But why would he do it?" she asked. "Why would he kill her?"

"I'm guessing it's because she made it hard for him to break off the affair. She could have been threatening to tell your grandmother and ruin his life. Sadie could get a little feisty sometimes."

"But…" Olivia stopped. This was a delicate subject. "From what I've heard, she was intimate with other men in town. It wasn't just my grandfather."

Randy pursed his lips in a grimace. "Yeah, she had plenty of affairs, but we always worked through them. She fell hard for Mario though, which is why I believed she'd run off to New York when their relationship came to an end. I figured she couldn't bear to be in the same town as him if she couldn't be with him. It hurt me a lot, but I got over it eventually, and I filed for divorce on the grounds of desertion after she'd been gone seven years." He shook his head. "I never believed she was dead. That came as a shock."

"Who are the other men she was close to?" Olivia asked tentatively. "Do you remember?"

His temper now rose along with his voice. "That's not your business. What does it matter after thirty years?"

"It matters because they might have information that would help me uncover the truth. I was attacked last night in my café, and it's related to your wife's murder."

A man's voice floated over Randy's head. "Dad, what's going on? Are you arguing with somebody?"

Randy turned in the doorway. His son, Bobby, was descending the stairs, dressed in shorts and a T-shirt. He was a carbon copy of his slight father, with thick dark hair and deep-set eyes. When he saw Olivia over Randy's shoulder, he approached the door with a look of wariness.

"It's not a good idea for you to be here, Miss Moretti," he said. "Dad's really angry with your family right now. You should go home."

"I'm here to make some simple enquiries, Mr. Billingham," she said. "I don't want to cause trouble."

Randy took an aggressive step forward and Olivia instinctively retreated a little way down the path.

"If you don't want to cause trouble, you'll stop bothering us," Randy said, as Bobby stretched out an arm to hold his father back. "You overstepped with your personal questions."

Bobby steered his father to the side of the hallway.

"Calm down, Dad," the younger man said. "You won't help matters by losing your cool."

Randy held up his hands in submission. "Yeah, yeah, you're right." He gave Olivia the side-eye. "She riled me by asking for the names of Sadie's male companions. That's private information."

"I know this is a difficult time, Mr. Billingham," Olivia said, feeling herself losing control of the situation. "You must be hurting, but I am too. I'm the one who found your wife in the cellar. I'm truly sorry for your loss."

Randy patted his son on the shoulder, reassuring him with a smile.

"Give me a moment," he said to his son. "I'm perfectly calm now, and I'd like a private chat with Miss Moretti before she leaves."

He stepped out onto the porch, shut the door and lowered his voice.

"I'm trying to protect Bobby from learning hurtful things about Sadie," he said. "Bear already visited us this morning, asking intrusive questions about her past relationships. Bobby knows his stepmother had affairs, but he doesn't know the extent of it. I'm begging you to think of his feelings and stop interfering. He was twenty-one when Sadie disappeared, and it devastated him. He always hoped she might come back or get in touch someday. Now he's found out she was buried right here in Abbeywood, it's like losing her all over again. Please let him grieve in peace."

Olivia fell silent for a while. If there was one thing she understood, it was bereavement. The deaths of her grandfather and mother within three years of each other had taken their toll.

"Someone tried to hurt me last night," she said, shivering in the cold. "Could you at least tell me if you have any ideas about the identity of the culprit?"

"I don't know anything."

Randy's eyes darted between her and the ground. She suspected he could give her the names of plenty of potential culprits.

"Where were you last night?" she asked. "Did you go out?"

He gave a wry smile. "I was home all night in case you're accusing me of anything." He folded his arms. "Listen, Miss Moretti, there are a whole bunch of men who'd want to stop you uncovering their indiscretions with Sadie. Even the sheriff has got secrets to hide."

Olivia's eyes widened. "Bear had an affair with Sadie?"

"He sure did." Randy pointed to his left. "And Dennis Clark from the grocery store down the street was just about to get married when he had a brief fling with Sadie. He wouldn't want anybody digging up that kind of information, especially as his fiancée never discovered his cheating, and they've now been married for thirty-two years."

Olivia was briefly stunned into silence. Randy's attitude had quickly changed since she'd enquired about his whereabouts the previous night. Now he was giving up names easily, as if trying to throw suspicion onto others. Could he have something to hide? Whatever the reason for his newly loosened tongue, this information was useful. Bear had been involved with the murder victim. That surely represented a conflict of interest in the investigation.

"I hope you can now understand why it's not a good idea to meddle in the past," Randy said, heading back inside. "Some secrets are better off left where they are."

Olivia finally realized why the people in her life were repeatedly warning her against investigating this murder. She would be opening a very big can of worms. But if she did nothing, her grandfather would take the rap for a murder she was sure he hadn't committed.

"Please could you give me a few more names of Sadie's male companions?" She reached into her purse to pull out a pen and notepad. "Maybe you could write them down here."

Randy's voice turned hard again. "Sadie was involved with almost every man in town at one time or another," he said bitterly. "Start with the letter *A* in the phone book and work your way through."

With that, he went inside and slammed the door, leaving her standing in the rain with a sinking heart. She trudged back to her car at the curb and sat down inside it. Checking her phone, she saw several missed calls from her father and one from Cal. The whole town had been advised to stay at home while the floodwaters raged, and she knew Leonardo would be worried. But why would Cal call? They had no reason to talk to one another.

Olivia clicked her tongue in annoyance, wondering if her father had called Cal for help in locating her. The Morettis should be keeping him at a distance, not inviting him into their lives. The way her father extended such friendliness and acceptance toward Cal was infuriating. She didn't want to reward him for his attempt to steal her family's café. She was mad with him, and she intended to stay that way.

She pulled out onto the highway with her windshield wipers on the fast setting. The rain had been falling all day, and the overflowing drains were struggling to cope. Large puddles had collected on the sides of the road, and Olivia carefully avoided them by driving slowly and remaining alert. She found herself worrying about her journey home. What if North Bridge was out? That sometimes happened in times of severe flooding.

On her approach to the bridge, her worst fears were realized when she spotted a "BRIDGE CLOSED" sign tied to a steel girder. She came to a stop and groaned, seeing the river flowing across the surface, making this route impassable. She'd have to take a detour to the other side of town, where South Bridge was situated at a higher spot above the water. She put the car in reverse and began to back up. That's when she noticed the vehicle behind her, right on her tail. She pressed the brake, confused about why this driver wasn't using their headlights in the heavy rain.

Then, in a dazzling glare, the front lights of the vehicle were activated as it moved forward, hitting her small compact with enough force to propel her toward the flooded bridge. She screamed and pumped the brakes, willing her little car to hold its ground. But she was no match for the vehicle on her tail, so she tried to turn around instead. Yet there wasn't enough space or time to perform the maneuver, and she soon found herself being shunted into the swirling waters of the river as it cascaded across the bridge.

Her car suddenly lifted off its wheels and began to float. As she fumbled for her cell phone on the seat next to her, she realized with terror that she was being swept along with the current. In no time at all, the bridge was in her rear-view mirror and the raging water started to seep through the doors. She was in serious trouble.

THREE

Cal had been unable to track down Olivia. After knocking on Randy Billingham's door, he'd learned she'd already been and gone. Randy had been tetchy and unpleasant in their brief conversation, but that wasn't surprising. The last thing the guy needed after learning of his wife's murder was to be questioned by the probable killer's granddaughter. Most of the townsfolk believed in Mario's guilt, not just because he was often grouchy and rude but because Sadie's body had been hidden in the cellar of Moretti's.

Since North Bridge had flooded one hour ago, Cal was unable to safely cross, so he was driving along the riverside road, heading for South Bridge instead. He scanned the swollen river just in case anyone had accidentally driven into the water, while still watching the roads for any sign of Olivia's car. He told himself she was just fine, but a ball of worry refused to budge from his belly. As he grappled with his fears, his radio crackled to life on the dash, and he heard the voice of Linda, a 911 dispatcher at the emergency call center.

"Chief Mackenzie?" she said. "Are you there?"

He stopped the truck and picked up the receiver. "I'm here, Linda. What's up?"

"A call just came in from a woman whose car entered the

river at North Bridge. She's now somewhere in the water between North and South Bridge. I've dispatched one of your fire trucks and an ambulance to the general location. Your deputy says you're patrolling the area so you might be able to get a visual on the car. It's a red Honda Civic."

His heart leaped into his mouth. This sounded like Olivia's car. "Do you know the caller's name?"

"Olivia Moretti."

He rested his forehead in his hand as his breath left his body. "Is she still on the line?"

"The call ended abruptly about three minutes ago. I think she might've dropped the phone into the water. The line won't reconnect."

"I'm on it. I'll update the emergency services when I find her."

He placed the receiver back in its cradle and set off downstream. He'd passed North Bridge a few minutes ago, so he might possibly spot the car bobbing in the water. How on earth could Olivia be so careless as to end up in the flood? Or had she run into someone or something sinister? Whatever the reason for her situation, now was not the time to allocate blame. He had to find her and take her out of danger.

He tried to concentrate on the road ahead while also scanning the river for a flash of red in the swirling gray waters. In circumstances like this, a quick escape was vital to survival, but Olivia might not know this. Most people would feel safer remaining in the safety of their vehicle rather than jumping into a raging flood. On the other hand, if Olivia hadn't activated the electric window mechanism soon after entering the water, it would be too late by now. The electrics would've cut out, and she would be trapped in a car that would stay afloat for no longer than a few minutes at most.

Cal could see nothing other than the dull mass of river, and he couldn't stop himself imagining Olivia crying out for help, banging on the windows as the water rose around her. He gripped the wheel tight and offered up a prayer. Perhaps Olivia was doing the same. He knew she shared the same faith, although Mario had insisted on sitting on opposite sides of the church when their families worshipped.

Cal slammed on his brakes as his eye caught a glint of red metal wedged into the riverbank. He jumped from his truck and raced to the grassy edge. Olivia's car had smashed into an uprooted tree that had fallen into the water. The windshield was broken, as were the side windows, but the car was being held up by the strong branches. Water gushed through the shattered windows, and both airbags had been deployed. He couldn't see any sign of the driver.

"Olivia!" he yelled above the noise of the gushing water. "It's Cal. Shout out to me if you can!"

There was no answer. In a panic, he scaled the slope of the soggy riverbank, slipping and sliding on the soft soil until he landed on the huge trunk of the fallen tree. Then he made his way along the bark on hands and knees, ignoring the splinters lodging in his fingers as he rushed to reach the car as quickly as possible. Once he was close enough, he spotted Olivia. She was squashed against the door on the driver's side, still buckled into her seat. There was a small trickle of blood on her temple. The water level was just below her chin, and her eyes were closed. To get to her, he'd be forced to clamber over the branches that had pierced the windshield.

"Olivia!" he yelled again. "You gotta wake up."

There was no response. He pulled his cell from his pocket and placed a call to the emergency dispatch, updating them on the whereabouts of the car and his decision to go into the water. Of course, the dispatcher advised him to return to safety. He would've done the same thing if the roles were reversed. The fire truck was en route, and protocol required him to await its arrival while monitoring the situation from a safe distance. The truck's specialist equipment would have the necessary tools to conduct an effective rescue. Cal knew all about standard procedure—and he decided to ignore it.

He hung up the phone, took off his padded yellow jacket and laid it on the tree trunk. He knew it would quickly become waterlogged and weigh him down. Then he kicked the glass of the passenger window with his heavy boot, dislodging the shards until a clean entrance into the car was created. The vehicle shifted and creaked as the metal twisted against the tree in the water. There was a chance the car could become dislodged and continue its journey into the torrents. If this happened during his rescue, he would be trapped inside a sinking vehicle with an unconscious woman. He'd never be able to get her out while she was a dead weight. But he'd never leave her either. It was likely they'd both die in that situation.

Knowing the risks, he kept his eyes on Olivia and made his way inside.

Olivia couldn't make sense of her surroundings. She was bitterly cold and was pinned in place by some kind of pressure on her chest. A man was calling her name, tapping her face and pinching her cheeks. It sounded like Cal, but why would he be there with her? She couldn't remember what happened.

"Olivia," he said loudly in her ear. "Focus on my voice and do what I say. You need to get out of the car. Open your eyes."

She flickered her lids. Her head was hurting, and her mind swam with a recent memory of slamming hard into a tree. A branch had broken the windshield and she'd tried to evade it, but she must not have succeeded, since everything after that was a blank.

"What happened?" she muttered. "How did I get here?"

"Your car got caught in the flood," he said, feeling his way gently around her neck with his fingers, poking and prodding with soft tips. "An ambulance is on the way. Stay still while I check for bone fractures."

"I didn't just get caught in the flood." Her grogginess was lifting. "Somebody forced my car onto the bridge." She now remembered the glare of her attacker's headlights and the whirring strain of her car's engine as she tried to hold her ground. "He did it on purpose."

"Are you sure?" Cal asked as he unbuckled her seat belt. Her body rose up in the water without the security of the belt, but Cal held her fast. "The roads are empty."

She pushed against him, fully opening her eyes in determination.

"It's true," she said. "I was on my way home from Randy Billingham's house, and somebody must have followed me."

"Let's talk about it later. I'm worried the car is slipping. We need to get out."

Cal gripped her tightly with both his arms around her torso. She felt his warm breath on her neck, and it reminded her of how cold she was. The water was frigid, muddy and brown, swirling with debris washed from the riverbank. If Cal hadn't roused her from unconsciousness, she'd surely have died of hypothermia—if she hadn't drowned first. He attempted to pull her from the seat, but she couldn't move. Her ankle was trapped by the twisted foot pedals.

"I'm stuck, Cal. I can't move my left leg."

He plunged his hands into the water and clasped them around her knee. Then he pulled hard.

"Ow, no, stop," she shouted. "It hurts."

"Do you think you've broken a bone?"

"No." She jiggled her foot back and forth. It hurt where the pedal had crunched around it, but the pain wasn't severe—she was pretty sure it wasn't broken. "But my ankle is stuck beneath the gas pedal."

Olivia heard the frustration in Cal's sigh. Getting her out wasn't going to be easy. It might not even be possible.

"Get out," she said, pushing his chest. "It's not safe for you to be here. Get out of the water."

"I'm not going anywhere, Olivia."

She sighed, exasperated. "Don't be a martyr. If you leave now, you should be fine. But if the car moves downstream, you might not be able to escape."

He cupped a hand around her nape, half in, half out of the water. Despite the bitter temperature of the river, his palm radiated heat onto her skin, and she closed her eyes to enjoy the shot of warmth.

"I'm not leaving you here alone," he said. "So don't ask me again."

"Come on, Cal," she said, raising a smile. "Surely it's not worth risking yourself like this to get your hands on my café. I won't support the sale, even if you save my life."

Her attempt to lighten the mood fell flat, and she quickly realized she'd gone too far yet again, because Cal didn't seem to appreciate the joke. His mouth turned down at the corners and his face crumpled a little.

"I'm sorry," she said. "I didn't mean it. I just don't want to be the reason you get hurt."

The car groaned and creaked around them, shifting noticeably from its position. She reckoned it might now be too late for Cal to leave the vehicle, even if he agreed to.

"The car!" she exclaimed, as it turned sideways in the water, buffeted by a sudden and powerful surge. "It's moving."

With a crunch of metal, the crumpled hood dislodged itself from the enormous tree and began to float backward. As the branches were yanked back through the windshield, they dislodged their leaves and foliage, scattering them like confetti on the water's surface.

"Hold on," Cal said, grabbing her by the shoulders and holding her tight. "Do exactly what I say, okay?"

She wasn't going to argue with him. This was his area of expertise, and the situation called for teamwork. "Okay."

"I'll be right back."

He took a deep breath and slid beneath the water as the car turned and swirled with the current. The hood was dipping lower and lower in the river, and Olivia was forced to stretch out her neck to keep breathing. Surely this was not how she was going to die? And what about Cal? She could only hope he'd make it out alive instead of paying the price for having come to her aid.

He popped up beside her and took a lungful of air. "I yanked the pedal, and your ankle is free. Take my hand and don't let go."

She did as he asked, and he pushed her through the window feetfirst. Her sweatshirt and jeans were heavy from all the water they'd absorbed, so she wasn't buoyant. As soon as she was out of the car, she tried to kick upward yet sunk downward. Thankfully, Cal had kept hold of her hand throughout, preventing her sinking to the depths of the riverbed. As the car finally dipped below the waterline, he kicked his way through the window and pushed her upward before yelling out.

"Float on your back and let the current take you on the surface. Don't fight it."

Their hands had been torn apart by the force of the water, and she gasped and scrabbled in the torrents, trying her best to face upward and stay on the surface, even as her body was being pulled downward by her sodden clothes and sneakers. She was tired.

"I see car headlights on the bridge overhead," Cal yelled, fighting his way through the water to reach her while they were propelled downstream. "It must be the police."

Olivia felt euphoria at the words—but then the first gunshot rang out, and she felt nothing but terror.

The shots coming from the gunman on the bridge missed them, but not by much. As Cal got closer, he tried to focus on the lone man in black, standing at the bridge railings, holding a rifle or shotgun at his side, but he couldn't get a good look while being buffeted by the current. He managed to fight his way to Olivia's side and did his best to stop her from sinking. She was panicking and attempting to swim, which was an understandable instinct that all too often caused people to drown. Floating was the better option but was an unnatural sensation to most people when plunged into dangerous waters.

"Try to grab a bridge support!" he yelled, pushing her toward the edge of the river, where the current was calmer. "And hold tight."

Two shots were discharged in quick succession, creating thunderclaps overhead. Olivia screamed and ducked below the surface briefly. Cal yanked her above the waterline, and she emerged spluttering and gasping for air.

Using all his strength, he grasped her around the waist and kicked upward, keeping their heads out of the water until he reached the metal supports of the bridge. With his free hand, he managed to reach out, grasp a girder and hold on. The water was gushing past his body, trying to take Olivia with it, but she quickly found a spot to anchor herself next to him. There, they both clutched the metal posts, where they could also take advantage of the coverage offered by the concrete bridge above. The unseen gunman discharged two more shots into the water close by, causing Olivia to scream in fright and squeeze her eyes tightly shut.

"Don't be scared," Cal said, raising his voice to be heard above the water. "We'll get out of here."

She could only nod silently as her teeth chattered and her hands shook. The water was intensely cold and filled with all kinds of debris, like fallen trees, road signs and household trash. Cal had even seen dead cattle in some places. The river was an incredibly unsafe place to be at that moment.

"Listen," he said, worried about her paling color. "Help is coming. You see the siren lights in the distance?"

She nodded again.

Above their heads, an engine roared to life and revved hard. The gunman must've left his vehicle at the side of the bridge, and he was now fleeing the scene before the fire truck arrived. Cal listened with relief as the tires squealed on the wet asphalt and faded into the distance. Now all they had to do was wait for rescue. Cal unclipped a small flashlight from a keychain on his waistband and began to shine it onto the riverbank. Someone would be sure to see it. As he flicked the switch on and off, he remembered what Olivia had said about being deliberately forced into the water. And now a gunman had taken potshots at them. There was no doubt that somebody was targeting her—and this time, they hadn't been content to stop at just a warning.

"Do you know who pushed your car into the water?" he asked. "Any idea at all?"

"I didn't get a good look at him or his car. It happened too fast."

Her voice was weak and breathless, as if the effort of speaking was overwhelming. Glancing across at her face, he could see her eyelids drooping. He needed to keep her talking before she fell unconscious and lost her grip on the girder. He didn't think he had enough strength to hold his own weight as well as hers in these powerful currents.

"Listen to me, Olivia," he said, inching his way across the girder so that his shoulder touched hers. "I came looking for you this evening because I was worried about you. It has nothing to do with my offer to buy the café. I know we've never seen eye to eye, but I want you to be safe."

Amid her shivers, he heard her laugh, before she responded in a shaky voice.

"You sure pick your moments for a heart-to-heart, don't you, Cal?"

"This is as good a time as any, right?" He felt his own breath now grow ragged, as the cold felt like it gnawed its way into his bones. "I mean, who hasn't forged a connection with an arch nemesis while they're both clinging to life in a raging flood?"

She laughed again, and he was pleased to see her shift her position to gain a better grip on the metal. She wasn't giving up just yet. He continued to blink his flashlight on and off as the blue and red lights of the fire truck came closer. He felt certain his colleagues would be able to see his signal in the dying light of the day.

"I don't know what we have going on between us, Cal," Olivia said. "But I wouldn't call it a connection."

"What would you call it?"

"A contention," she said, without missing a beat. "It sounds a lot like connection but has a completely different meaning. I think you just confused the two words."

He smiled. Even in these treacherous conditions, Olivia's sharp mind hadn't been blunted.

"I don't want to be in contention with you, Olivia," he said. "Don't you think this feud has gone on long enough?"

"What do you want me to do, Cal?" she asked. "You want me to step aside so you can buy my café without feeling guilty?"

He thought about this while battling to maintain his grip. "I want you to realize that if your dad doesn't sell it to me, then he could end up selling to someone who might not respect the history of the place. I'm not the bad guy here." He paused. "I don't want to be the reason you get hurt."

"Those are the exact words I said to you when you came to my rescue a few minutes ago."

Cal cast his mind back. She was right. She had been trying to protect him from danger by encouraging him to leave the car before it slipped back into the swollen river. She had been willing to die alone rather than allow him to risk his life. If Olivia was prepared to make that kind of sacrifice, then he should consider being as humble in return.

"If I'm hurting you, I want to make it right," he said, hearing the tires of the fire truck come to a stop on the bridge above. "What can I do?"

"Withdraw your offer," she said, stopping momentarily to catch her breath. "And leave my café alone. Why can't you start afresh with a new café? Why do you have to take Moretti's?"

He watched her close her eyes and rest her forehead on the metal post in front of her as she hugged it tightly with both arms. Her long hair was flowing in the current, the curls stretched out by the weight of the water. She appeared so exhausted and sad that he wanted to do anything to ease her pain. Despite her hostility toward him over the years, she was still a person who deserved compassion. He thought of his grand plans to open a chain of cafés across the state, and of the certainty he'd felt when offering to purchase Moretti's.

"I love the place," he answered honestly. "I want to preserve its heritage and atmosphere. When I heard it was facing serious money worries, I knew I wanted to save it."

"*I* can save it," she said strongly. "Just trust me on that."

She sounded so certain that he believed her.

"Okay," he relented. "I'll talk to your father to ask him if he'll allow me to withdraw from the sale. I'll find someplace else."

It didn't sit right with Cal to renege on the proposal before discussing it with Leonardo. Leonardo was the decision-maker for Moretti's, and Cal respected him too much to simply walk away without a conversation.

Olivia said nothing but turned to look at him with a weak smile. He was just about to take off his belt and use it to securely attach her to the bridge support when one of his colleagues dropped into view a few feet away. It was Vinny, the youngest member of the emergency response team, and he was clipped onto the end of a winch cable, his feet dangling just above the raging waterline.

"Hi, boss," the young man called out. "We saw your flashlight signal." He held a harness in the air. "Who's getting the first ride up?"

Cal pointed to Olivia. "Take good care of her, Vinny. She's had a really bad day."

* * *

Olivia sat at her kitchen table, feeling as though she was attending a job interview. Her father was seated opposite with Cal, and on either ends of the table were Rosalie and the Abbeywood Church pastor, Brian Caulfield. Leonardo had arranged the meeting after waiting a couple of days for Olivia to recover from her river ordeal. Her mild concussion was now resolved, and she felt like her old self again. Yet her dad was worried about her, and he'd called these people together to conduct a discussion about the current situation. Not only was he anxious about the attacks on his daughter, but he'd grown concerned about the increasing animosity Olivia was displaying toward Cal. Olivia felt unsettled. Cal wouldn't look her in the eye, despite her trying to force it.

Beneath the table, Rosalie patted Olivia's knee, and the best friends smiled at one another. Rosalie was wearing a T-shirt on which the phrase *Hang in There* was written beneath a picture of a cat clinging to a tree branch. It was a message of support, and Olivia appreciated it.

"Thank you all for coming," Leonardo said after Pastor Brian completed his opening blessing. "And thank you for the prayers and good wishes you've offered my family these past few difficult days. Olivia's been through a lot, and we're gathered here to help her."

Murmurs resounded around the table and Olivia acknowledged the kindness with a smile.

"I'm fine," she reassured them. "You don't need to worry."

Pastor Brian leaned on the table with his elbows. A portly man of fifty-seven, his round face radiated love and gentleness.

"Whatever danger you're facing, you have your church family behind you," he said. "And let's praise God for placing Cal at the right place at the right time to wake you from unconsciousness and help you escape from the car before it sank." The pastor looked between Cal and Olivia. "We're proud of you both for working together and evading the gunman. It's not often we see teamwork from you guys."

Cal smiled awkwardly. He seemed uncomfortable, as if he didn't want to be there, and Olivia was uncertain why. After all, he was the hero of the hour.

"Thank you, Cal," she said. "Despite our difficult history, you were there when I needed you, and I'm grateful."

"That brings me to my next point," Pastor Brian said. "I've been pastoring to the Morettis and the Mackenzies for more than twenty years, and during that time, I've been unable to bridge the divide between the two families. When Mario passed away six years ago, I thought the feud might die with him, but it's sadly continued with the younger generation." He glanced between Cal and Olivia again. "But the time has come to move forward in a spirit of reconciliation and forgiveness. Let's end this historic quarrel once and for all. Leonardo told me the situation has gotten worse lately. Since Cal made an offer to purchase Moretti's, some unkind words have been spoken."

Olivia bowed her head, feeling slightly shamefaced because, between her and Cal, she was the more hostile. After Mario died, Cal's parents, Roger and Susan, had approached her after a church service and invited her to dinner. They'd hoped to start afresh now that the main instigator of the conflict was gone. Yet Olivia had been too loyal to her grandfather's memory to be able to move past her distrust of her business rivals. Mario had instilled in her a belief that the Mackenzies were always looking for sneaky ways to copy Moretti's menu, style and ambience. Hence, she had declined their offer and continued to keep her distance.

Her father had gone to the Mackenzies' dinner party alone. Pastor Brian was now forcing her to question whether she'd made the right decision. Her father had begun to socialize with Cal's parents regularly since Mario's death, so it really was only Olivia who sustained the animosity. But now that Cal had saved her twice, she was starting to realize that she'd been unfair to spend so much time assuming the worst of him.

"I guess you have a point," Olivia said, her head still bowed. "Nonno's dislike of the Mackenzies rubbed off on me a little too much, and Cal's offer to purchase Moretti's Café brought it all to the fore." She lifted her head and smiled at Cal. "But now he's agreed to back out of the sale, I think I can let the hostility go and move on."

Cal, wearing his fire chief's uniform of black pressed pants and a short-sleeved shirt, continued to avoid her eye, and her stomach began to sink. She sensed she was about to be hit with bad news.

"Cal asked me if he could withdraw his offer because of your objection to it," her father said. "But I'd like to go through with the sale. I spoke to a Realtor yesterday about putting Moretti's on the open market, and he told me the murder scandal has affected its value. Cal's offer is probably the highest one we'll receive. I'm thankful he's prepared to honor it."

Olivia stared at Cal, open-mouthed. "So you're going ahead with the purchase, huh? Even after everything you said to me while we were in the water."

"I meant every word," Cal said, finally looking at her. "But your dad says Moretti's will go bankrupt without a buyer, and I want your family to get the full value for it. If I'm the only one prepared to offer what it's worth, then isn't that the offer your family should take?"

She switched her attention to her father, still stuck on the first part of what Cal had said. "We'll go bankrupt? I thought we only had a few cash flow issues."

"It's more serious than you think, especially since we've had to close because of the flooding and won't be able to reopen without expensive repairs." Leonardo looked at her sadly. "We have enough cash to continue for one month, maybe two. After that, the mortgage company will foreclose, and Moretti's will be forced to shut its doors for good. Cal's buyout will preserve its legacy."

She gasped. "Why didn't you tell me this before now?"

"Because I was hoping to find a way to raise the capital we need," he replied. "I didn't want to worry you until I'd exhausted all avenues." He looked between her and Rosalie. "I know we only have a small staff, but I've been trying to safeguard everyone's jobs. Cal has promised that nobody will get laid off."

"The café is always busy," Rosalie said. "Olivia and I are flat out most days. I don't understand why this is happening."

"She's right, Dad," Olivia chimed in. "If you let me take over the books, I can set us on an even keel. Why don't we try it out before selling?"

"This is my decision, Olivia," her father said. "And it's final. I know you'll be hurt and angry, but I don't want you to take it out on Cal. That's part of the reason I called the meeting. You should agree to put your old rivalry with Cal behind you. Your grandfather was the cause of it all, and he's been gone six years. Let's move on."

"I can't believe this is happening," Olivia said, focusing on the most important issue to her—the sale of Moretti's. "I always thought Moretti's Café would stay in the family forever. How did it all go so wrong? Not only is Nonno accused of being a murderer but we're about to sell his café to a Mackenzie. He'd be turning in his grave right now." She raked her fingers through her hair in frustration. "This is like a nightmare."

Rosalie reached for Olivia's hand, and the friends gripped each other's fingers tightly. Only Rosalie truly understood the anguish Olivia felt, because they shared everything. Olivia had cried on Rosalie's shoulder after the death of both her mother and grandfather. Rosalie knew of Olivia's deep-seated loyalty to Mario.

"It's not a nightmare, Olivia," Leonardo said calmly. "It's an opportunity to move forward with our lives and put your grandfather's mistakes behind us."

Olivia assumed she knew the mistake her father was referring to.

"Nobody knows who killed Sadie," Olivia said, coming to her grandfather's defense. "It could've been anybody."

"The poor woman was bricked in the cellar of Moretti's Café thirty years ago," Leonardo said. "Who do you think put her there if not your grandfather?"

"Somebody could've stolen a key to the café," Olivia said. "A supplier or a member of staff maybe?"

Leonardo clicked his tongue. "Do you really think your grandfather wouldn't have noticed a false wall appearing overnight in his cellar?"

"*You* didn't notice it," she shot back. "It was very well concealed."

Pastor Brian held up his hands placatingly. "I think we're heading off track. Emotions are running high and it's easy to let them overwhelm us. What happened to Sadie Billingham is tragic, but we cannot make it better by allocating blame or turning on each other. God knows what happened and only He can judge."

"Hear, hear," Leonardo agreed. "I'm sorry for lashing out, Olivia. I just want you to understand that you're placing herself at risk by digging into Sadie's past. I'm so worried for your safety."

The pastor nodded vigorously. "Yes, Olivia's safety is one of the church's priorities right now. I've already set up a daily prayer circle for this specific matter, and I've secured Cal's agreement to be her protector whenever she wants to take a trip out of the house."

"What?" Olivia looked between Cal and Pastor Brian. "Like a babysitter?"

"Like a friend and helper," the pastor corrected. "Cal's already proven himself to be very capable when it comes to guarding you, and if you spend a little more time together, I'm sure it will heal the family rift." He smiled. "There's a deep bond between you two that's waiting to emerge. I just know it." He linked his two index fingers together. "All it takes is a little teamwork."

Olivia laughed uncomfortably. "It's a nice vision, but Cal is busy right now with the flooding situation."

"I have some time to spare in between my duties," Cal said. "As long as you give me a little notice. If I'm unavailable, Brian has a list of congregation members who'll step up."

"Oh!" It looked like Cal was fully on board with the plan and she didn't want to seem ungrateful. "It's all been worked out, huh?"

"Does that mean you agree?" the pastor asked hopefully. "I won't force your hand on this. It's your decision."

"Please, Olivia," her father implored. "It would put my mind at rest to know that you're protected."

Olivia tilted her head at her old adversary. "Do you think this arrangement could work, Cal?"

He shrugged. "Sure. I want to help out as much as I can."

She saw the pleading look in her father's eyes and relented.

"All right. I guess it's okay by me," she said. "Until the guy is caught anyways."

Leonardo clapped his hands together and rubbed. "Great. This calls for some celebratory coffee and Olivia's famous panettone." He pushed back his chair. "Maybe you can give me a hand, Cal?"

While the three men busied themselves in the kitchen, Rosalie reached for her friend's hand.

"You okay, Liv?" she asked quietly. "You probably feel like everybody's telling you how to live your life."

"Exactly." Rosalie was always perceptive. "It's frustrating."

"You know it's because they want to keep you safe, right? Sometimes, you can be a little…" She stopped speaking, searching for the best descriptor.

"Impulsive?" Olivia suggested.

Rosalie smiled. "I love you with all my heart, but occasionally you act first and think later." She glanced at Cal, who was setting panettone on a plate while Leonardo put mugs on a tray. "Let them take care of you while you need it. You might end up being thankful for it."

Olivia gave Rosalie's hand an extra tight squeeze. All too often, Olivia was hasty in her decisions and regretful later. Having to call Cal to organize an outing would ensure she considered her trips carefully. It was probably for the best. But spending time with him might prove difficult. She wasn't sure why he'd agreed to the arrangement in the first place. He probably felt guilty about buying the café out from under her and was seeking a way to ease his conscience. Not that it mattered to Olivia. She intended on finding a way to save the café herself. All she needed was a brilliant plan to suddenly occur to her.

This fight wasn't over. Not by a long shot.

FOUR

The forest landslide contained a mix of water, soil, rock and uprooted trees. Cal stood at the foot of the slurry, shaking his head and sighing. This was the last thing the town needed, but it was hardly a surprising occurrence. Rain was continuing to fall across the county and the Abbeywood Forest had taken a drenching. The slide happened quickly during the night, shifting about half an acre of hillside downward, where loggers had cut down a section of trees. As these large trees had previously sucked moisture from the ground, their removal had led to the soil becoming saturated and unstable.

Cal conducted a risk assessment of the slide, carefully making his way around the liquefied bowl of earth that had pooled at the bottom. Thankfully, the flow had stopped a good distance from the road, but he'd need to monitor the situation at least once a day to ensure the ground held firm. His list of duties was increasing but he was still committed to finding time for Olivia whenever she wanted to leave the house. He'd agreed to accompany her on outings because Brian had made such an impassioned plea. The pastor seemed to think the arrangement would allow them to become friends and heal the old divide. Cal wasn't so sure. Only time would tell.

As well as monitoring the mudslide, Cal was also tasked with keeping a close eye on the flood defenses at the Redwood Reservoir. The reservoir supplied the homes of Abbeywood with water and had been created fifty-five years ago by building a dam across the Redwood River. The reservoir's earth dam had developed numerous cracks over the years but had remained structurally sound so far. However, this latest rainfall was causing these cracks to widen. If the dam failed, hundreds of people would be at risk from escaping water. If necessary, he'd have to advise the mayor to issue an evacuation order for those living in Redwood Estates and the surrounding valley. Despite him contacting the dam owners several times, they had failed to respond with anything other than vague promises of action. The State Dam Safety Office was snowed under with issues caused by the flooding and had not yet conducted an inspection. This meant the responsibility currently fell to Cal.

No matter how burdened Cal felt, he'd promised Pastor Brian he would be there for Olivia if she needed him. Whenever possible, he could work late into the evening or early in the morning and allocate time to her in between. It was clear she wouldn't halt her investigation into Sadie's murder, no matter the personal cost. He'd been racking his brains to think of who might be capable of carrying out these attacks on her. Cal had always assumed Abbeywood was a safe town and its residents were good people, but he'd been forced to reassess his opinions. Somebody was determined to stop Olivia from poking around into the past, and that person might stop at nothing to ensure her silence.

A voice broke through his thoughts.

"Hey there, Cal." He looked up to see Bear heading his way, taking a detour around the mud. "What a mess, huh?" He looked skyward. "At least it's not raining."

Cal grimaced. "I wouldn't get used to the dry weather. It won't last."

The sheriff took off his hat and rubbed his bushy hair. "This is getting really worrying. I've just come from the Redwood Reservoir. If we see a lot more rain, the dam might not hold out."

"Believe me, I know," Cal said with a sigh. "Let's take it one problem at a time. What did you find out about the river attack on Olivia yesterday? Any leads?"

Bear shook his head. "I got nothing to go on. She didn't notice the make, model or color of the vehicle that pushed her into the river. And the guy who shot at you from the bridge is just a shadowy man in black."

"I'm pretty sure he was using a rifle," Cal said. "And the weapon recovered from the café was a shotgun. I think he might be a hunter."

"Well, there are plenty of those around here." Bear shrugged his big shoulders beneath his sheriff's jacket. "What's happening to Olivia is terrible, but she's not making life easy for me. I've received a couple of anonymous complaints about her phone calls to local people. I'm guessing they don't want to leave a name because they're embarrassed about their past relationships with Sadie."

He hooked his thumbs into his belt loops, where his belly strained slightly beneath his shirt.

"But I've now received an official complaint from someone who *did* leave his name—Randy Billingham. Olivia's acting like a law enforcement officer and it's not right. I feel I have no choice other than to issue her a warning later today. If she continues to pester the Billinghams, I might have to cite her."

Cal narrowed his eyes at Bear. He'd known the sheriff his whole life, and this hostile attitude was unusual. Bear was known as a gentle giant, firm but fair in all matters. It made Cal wonder what had prompted this change. Was Bear possibly afraid of what Olivia's questions might reveal?

"What do you remember about Sadie?" Cal asked. "You must've known about her affair with Mario, right? Apparently, it was the worst-kept secret in Abbeywood."

"Yeah, I knew about Sadie and Mario, but I kept my nose out of their business. Adultery isn't against the law."

"When she vanished, didn't anybody from her family report her as a missing person?"

"I don't think anyone was all that surprised that she left. No one thought to suspect foul play. Sadie had a difficult life, and she had no family to speak of except for Randy and Bobby. She grew up in foster homes in Concord, being bounced around the system until she met Randy when she was working in a strip joint at the age of nineteen. She was a damaged person, looking for love in all the wrong places, and Randy was definitely one of those wrong places. He supplied her with drink and drugs to numb the pain instead of getting her into therapy." Bear looked off into the distance wistfully. "That poor woman never had a chance in life. She could've been happy, but she was never going to find that happiness here, trapped in an unhealthy marriage and a one-sided love affair. Some of us…well, we hoped that she'd found some kind of peace in a fresh start somewhere new."

Cal watched the moisture collect in the sheriff's eyes. This was clearly personal.

"Sounds like you knew Sadie well, Bear," he said. "Were you good friends?"

The reply came quickly. "No. I just felt sorry for her."

"Did you have many interactions with her? Did she ever fall on the wrong side of the law?"

"I never arrested her if that's what you mean." The shake of Bear's head was a little too emphatic and he seemed uncomfortable with this line of questioning. "I'd better get going. I only came to check on the landslide, but I see you have it all under control."

"I'll let you know if it heads further toward the road," Cal called after Bear's retreating figure. He was in a rush to leave. "Thanks for checking on the reservoir."

The sheriff waved a hand as he entered the thicket of trees. Cal stood there for a few moments, pondering their conversation. Cal and Bear had been close friends and colleagues for many years, despite the twenty-year age difference, and Cal trusted the sheriff with his life. But there was no doubt that Bear was spooked. Was he hiding his own affair with Sadie?

It was just another worry to add to Cal's ever-growing pile.

Olivia drove slowly along the riverside road, singing at the top of her voice to keep the flashbacks at bay. The raging river reminded her of being cold and scared, clinging to the metal posts of the bridge with Cal by her side. She tried to shake her head free of Cal's face. She certainly didn't need reminding of his unwelcome intrusion into her life, in more ways than one. But she was still resolved to keep him out of the café, no matter what. Since her father had informed her of his decision to accept Cal's buyout offer, she'd been exploring the ways in which she could prevent the deal going ahead. She'd applied for a loan at the bank and was hopeful of an interview with the manager. If she was approved, she could purchase Moretti's herself. Then she could set about taking control of the accounts and making the place profitable again.

Gripping her hands tightly onto the steering wheel, she navigated the roadside puddles and told herself that everything would be fine, despite her coming out alone that day. She'd thought long and hard about calling Cal to ask him to accompany her but had decided against it. She needed to ask Bear some tough questions and, considering Bear and Cal were good friends, Cal was bound to take the sheriff's side. It would be easier to make this journey alone, and since she'd be with the sheriff, she wasn't concerned for her safety. She wouldn't be out long anyway. Her father had taken her grandmother out on a walk, so Olivia only had an hour to spare. Leonardo often wheeled Francesca around the neighborhood to keep her in touch with her surroundings, and Olivia had borrowed his car while he was gone. But he needed it back on his return to get to an appointment. Hence, she planned on making this trip a quick one.

She turned right onto Crescent Hill, where the sheriff's office was situated high above the river. While most businesses and stores had been forced to close because of the floods, including the Moretti's and Mackenzie's cafés, a few fortunate places remained open due to their safe locations. The sheriff's office was among them.

Pulling into the parking lot, she saw Bear exiting his vehicle, as if he'd just returned from patrol. It was perfect timing, as she could confront him while he was alone. This was a very delicate subject to tackle and she was sure Bear wouldn't want to be overheard.

"Ah, Olivia," Bear said, on seeing her pull up next to him and slide down her window. "I need to speak with you."

"That's a coincidence," she said, stepping out of her father's car. "Me too. Shall I go first?" Before he could object, she asked her question without warning. "Did you have an affair with Sadie Billingham?"

Bear's eyes widened in surprise. He plainly hadn't been expecting her to ask about such a personal subject, and he was unprepared. He opened and closed his mouth repeatedly, struggling to formulate a response. Finally, it seemed that he decided the truth was the only option.

"Yes," he said quietly. "I had a short relationship with Sadie when I was a twenty-one-year-old deputy, but it was never serious. She was eighteen years older than me, and I was young and stupid. I broke it off about a year before she disappeared."

At last, Olivia felt she was getting somewhere in her investigation. This was the kind of useful information she'd been seeking.

"Were you seeing her at the same time she was having an affair with my grandfather?"

Bear looked at the floor. "Yes, I was, but she was besotted with Mario. She was only using me to make him jealous. He refused to leave your grandmother, but she thought she could change his mind. Like I said, I was young and stupid, and I've regretted it ever since."

Olivia crossed her arms. "Don't you think this represents a conflict of interest in your investigation into Sadie's murder?"

Bear took a step backward as his expression grew hostile.

"A conflict of interest?" he repeated. "What exactly are you saying?"

"There might be facts you want covered up," she replied, emboldened by his admission. "You're not an impartial investigator."

"I am totally impartial," he said, raising his voice. "No matter what happened between me and Sadie, I'm an officer of the law, and I swore an oath to uphold the values of the badge. Of course I'd rather the townsfolk didn't know about my relationship with a married woman, but even if that should come out, it won't stop me from doing my job and investigating this crime in the same way I'd investigate any other."

"As far as I can tell, Bear, you're not conducting an investigation at all," she challenged. "You think it's an open-and-shut case and you haven't even looked at any suspects other than my grandfather."

"That's not fair," Bear said, raising his face to the sky in apparent frustration. "I've conducted interviews with Sadie's husband, stepson and her friends, and I've tracked her last known movements. In the days leading up to her disappearance, she shared with several people that she was threatening to expose her affair with Mario to your grandmother. Then she ends up dead and hidden in the cellar of Moretti's." He threw up his hands. "Just accept it. Your grandfather could be charming when he wanted to be, and I know he cared for you a great deal, but there was more to him than the side he showed you. He was also a liar, a cheater and probably a killer. I had nothing against him personally, I'm simply telling it like it is. He had means, motive, opportunity and a very close tie to the place where the body was found. There's no good reason to suspect anyone else. If you keep poking, you might uncover some more dirty secrets, but you're not going to be able to clear Mario's name. The only thing you'll accomplish by chasing shadows will be getting yourself hurt."

Olivia stood in silence for a few moments. Hearing her grandfather described in this awful way hit like a gut punch. Bear would never normally speak this harshly to her, but it was no surprise he was defensive in the face of her accusations. After all, she had landed the first blow.

"Listen to me, Olivia," Bear said, softening his tone. "I've received a complaint about your harassment of Randy Billingham and his son, Bobby. I'm officially ordering you to stop. Lots of people are worried about you. You shouldn't even be out here by yourself." He opened the door to his cruiser. "I'll escort you home."

"No." The way Bear had casually called her grandfather a killer still rung in her ears. "I'll make my own way home."

"Don't be foolish," he said. "Let me lead the way. Nobody will mess with you if they see my cruiser up front."

She opened her driver's door and sat behind the wheel. At that moment, she wanted to be nowhere near Bear.

"I'll be fine," she said, closing the door and starting up the engine.

She backed out of the lot and turned onto the highway, watching Bear's large figure growing ever smaller in her rearview mirror. Until recently, she had assumed the sheriff was one of the good guys. Now she didn't know what to think.

As she mulled over these facts, she noticed a car approaching at high speed from behind. She made the decision to pull over and let it pass but before she could activate her blinker, the car rammed her bumper with such a force that she almost lost control, skidding on the slick surface of the highway. As soon as she righted herself, she pressed the gas pedal to the floor in an effort to take herself away from the danger, while fumbling on the passenger seat for her cell phone.

"Oh no," she said aloud as she remembered watching her car slip beneath the swirling water of the river two days ago, taking her purse with it. "No cell phone."

Another bump from behind sent her skipping forward, but she maintained control and flicked her eyes between the road ahead and the rearview mirror, reminding herself to notice as many details as possible. She wanted to be able to give a better description of her attacker this time.

The car on her tail was black, with two distinctive white stripes on the hood. She'd never seen it before, and the person behind the wheel was impossible to identify, wearing a baseball cap and sunglasses and with scarf wound tightly around his face. Her chest hammered as adrenaline coursed through her veins. She was driving her father's old Buick and the car nudging her bumper appeared to be powerful and sporty. She was outmatched.

Glancing to her right, she saw the swirling gray mass of the river rushing by. She didn't want to end up in there again. Taking a sharp left-hand turn, she traveled down a farm track, a shortcut to the mountain road, which would take her toward Abbeywood Forest. From a high location, there was no danger of ending up in the river, and maybe she could find some loggers to help her. She splashed through the deep puddles that had collected on the dirt road, occasionally hitting a pothole, causing the car to jolt upward. As she flicked her eyes between the mirror and the track, she didn't notice the discarded tractor tire in front of her until it was too late. She tried to swerve around it, but an impact was unavoidable. Her left wheel clipped the obstruction, and the car juddered violently, before skidding and performing a complete U-turn.

She came to an abrupt stop with an involuntary scream and found herself facing her pursuer. Their hoods were nose to nose, both cars motionless. Olivia's breath came quick and heavy, while her mind raced to formulate a plan. But she drew a blank.

The black car revved hard, inching its way forward until it began nudging her backward. She quickly moved the stick into reverse and floored the gas pedal, twisting her whole body around to navigate the track backward. Yet still her pursuer kept coming, staying right on her hood until she burst out onto the quiet mountain road with a squeal of tires. Fortunately, she ended up facing the right direction again, and she focused on the way ahead. She ascended the hillside as fast as possible, praying that someone, anyone, would be there to help her escape the threat.

Cal was taking detailed photographs of the mudslide when the sound of vehicles on the mountain road disturbed him. He lifted his ear and listened. It appeared that two cars were racing each other, and the noise of their whirring and straining engines caught on the wind. He clicked his tongue in annoyance. Even though the rainfall had briefly abated, the asphalt on local roads was still slick, meaning that traveling at high speeds came with extra risks right now. Cal knew, firsthand, the tragedy of high-speed collisions. He'd cut far too many reckless young men out of mangled vehicles after they'd miscalculated a bend in the road. Most of them made full recoveries, but the less fortunate ones never made it home.

"Slow down," he muttered, returning to his task of photographing the slide. "What's the rush?"

But neither car adjusted their speed, and the sound of their engines only grew louder as they came ever closer. Cal was too far from the road to go lecture these drivers. All he could do was pray they made it home safely. The sudden and piercing squeal of tires indicated that one of the vehicles had ground to a halt at the side of the road, possibly close to where he'd left his truck on the shoulder. Pocketing his camera, he waited for more sounds to reach him, and when they did, his blood ran cold.

It was Olivia. And she was screaming his name.

In an instant, he took off running, slipping and sliding on the mud in his haste to reach her.

"Olivia!" he yelled as he ran into the forest. "Run toward my voice."

"Cal!" she shouted in response. "I can't see you."

In the cover of the forest, the thick trunks acted like barriers, bouncing sounds around and making it difficult to assess their location. Cal took out his flashlight and aimed the beam into the treetops. Under the darkness of the red oaks and sugar maples, the beam was easily seen, like a searchlight at sea.

"Follow the light," he called. "Look up."

Her response gave him instant relief. "I see it. I'm heading your way."

When she came into view, his first thought was to hold his arms out wide. He knew from the look on her face that she was terrified. It must've been the terror that propelled her into his embrace, because she wasn't usually tactile with him. Yet she flung her arms around his neck to hold tight, while fighting for breath.

"I was followed," she managed to say. "I saw your truck, so I stopped and ran into the forest." She glanced over her shoulder. "I don't know where the other car went. I don't hear it."

He unwound her arms from around his neck and reached into his pocket to pull out a small black device. It was a mobile siren that he sometimes used to attract the attention of his men in chaotic firefighting situations.

Handing it to her, he said, "Press this button if you feel unsafe. I'm going to look for this guy, but I'll come right back if you activate the siren, okay?"

He headed off into the forest, scanning all directions, as

the sound of birdsong punctuated the sky overhead. Then he heard a squeal of tires, as if a car was racing away from the roadside. He spotted Olivia's footprints in the thick mud. Following the trail, it led him all the way to her car, which was parked right behind his truck on the shoulder. The driver's door was still open, and the car was emitting a beeping sound as a reminder to close it. There was no sign of the guy or his vehicle, but he hadn't left the scene without sending Olivia a stark warning.

Written in red letters on her windshield were the words *LET THE DEAD SLEEP OR YOU'LL JOIN THEM.*

Cal rubbed the greasy words on the glass with a cloth, but the lipstick proved difficult to remove. Rather than wiping away, it smeared across the surface. He walked to his truck to get some detergent wipes from his glove box, noticing Olivia pick up the discarded lipstick from the ground.

"This is an old brand of makeup," she said. "You can't buy it anymore."

After retrieving the wipes, Cal returned to the task of removing the words from the windshield. He'd already taken numerous photographs from several angles to show to Bear later.

"Why would a guy have lipstick in his car?" Cal wondered. "Are you sure it was a man who followed you?"

"I'm pretty sure," she replied. "Maybe it was his wife's car. I don't know the model, but it's old like this lipstick." She placed the tube on the roof of her father's tan Buick and let out a huge sigh. "My dad's gonna miss his appointment because I'll be late home with his car."

"I thought someone was supposed to accompany you when you go out," Cal said. "We agreed on it, right? You didn't need to borrow your dad's car. I would've picked you up."

"I was just going to the sheriff's office," she said. "I figured I'd be safe while I was there, and since it's not a long drive, I wasn't expecting to run into any trouble on the way there or back."

He stopped wiping the glass and focused on her. "I still wish you'd called me. If I'd been with you, maybe this wouldn't have happened."

"I had to go alone—because I went to see Bear," she said, finally looking remorseful. "I didn't tell you because I thought you'd take his side."

"Take his side? What do you mean? Did you two argue?"

Olivia avoided his eye as she recounted her conversation with the sheriff, telling Cal about Sadie's affair with Bear more than thirty years ago. Cal now understood why the sheriff had seemed awkward earlier. He was obviously embarrassed about his relationship with a married woman.

"I don't think we can trust Bear to be unbiased," Olivia said. "I think he's more interested in keeping Sadie's affairs covered up and avoiding gossip than actually finding out what happened."

Cal physically balked. Sure, Bear was being a little harsher than usual with Olivia, but he was still a decent man and a good sheriff. He wouldn't ignore a serious threat just to protect himself from embarrassment.

"That's highly unlikely," he said, keeping his voice level and reminding himself not to scoff at the idea, no matter how far-fetched he found it. He knew he had to tread carefully with Olivia. She was close to the edge with all the pressures currently heaped on her.

"Bear's relationship with Sadie doesn't prove he had anything to do with her murder," he continued, removing the last trace of lipstick from the windshield. "You have to trust him right now, because you need him. We should report this latest incident immediately."

"No."

He clicked his tongue. "Sometimes I think you choose to ignore my advice just because I'm a Mackenzie."

Olivia folded her arms and adopted a combative pose, with her chin lifted high. She didn't know how to do anything other than disagree with him. Mario had instilled in her a strong dislike of the Mackenzie family that was proving difficult to overcome.

"Pastor Brian asked us to put our rivalry behind us," he said. "We should at least try."

Olivia relaxed her shoulders and sighed. "Yeah, I guess you're right. You've helped me out a lot recently." She dropped her voice, as if being nice to him required hushed tones. "I appreciate it. You're not so bad after all."

He took a step backward with an exaggerated look of surprise. "Wow. That was unexpected."

She punched him playfully. "Don't get used to it. Compliments aren't my strong point."

"Tell me about it."

They smiled at one another in silence, and Cal found himself enjoying a rare moment of peace with Olivia. But then he remembered her situation and returned to more pressing matters.

"Bear can potentially trace the vehicle that pursued you and locate the owner," he said. "There's a security camera at the bottom of the mountain road to monitor logging vehicles. He can request access to the footage."

Olivia was still reluctant. "He's hiding something about his relationship with Sadie, Cal. I know it."

Cal had a feeling she might be right, but he trusted Bear

nonetheless. Whatever the man was hiding, he wouldn't let it get in the way of doing his job and protecting the community.

"Think on it," he suggested. "And in the meantime, make sure to call me whenever you want to go out."

She groaned and kicked at a small stone, sending it bouncing across the asphalt.

"I hate having to rely on other people. I've always prided myself on being independent, taking care of things myself," she said. "I want things to go back to how they used to be."

He knew what she meant, knew that the attacks had scared her and made her aware of her vulnerability in the worst possible way. As badly as he wanted to, he knew he couldn't promise that she'd be safe from now on. But he *could* deliberately misunderstand her—and hopefully lift her mood for a minute. With that in mind, he flashed her a smile. "Back when I took every opportunity to tease you about our kiss?"

She laughed. "Yeah."

"It was a great kiss though. The best you've ever had, am I right?"

She shook her head, her eyes bright. "Don't flatter yourself, Cal. I barely remember it."

"You're a terrible liar."

She pursed her lips and tilted her head, daring him to continue. Usually, he'd persist in his teasing, enjoying the sparks it created, but today he decided to give her a break. He walked to her and stood close. Her hair had frizzed in the growing moisture of the morning and the weak sunlight shone through the strands, creating a halo-like effect. He felt a pull of attraction to her that took him off guard. He quashed it instantly.

"Whether you like it or not, you need help," he said, resuming a somber tone. "And you need Bear. I know you think the whole world is against you right now, but it's not true. I want to find out the identity of the man who's stalking you, and I want to see him brought to justice." He laid a hand on her shoulder. "We have to cooperate on this."

He saw her swallow hard, as if suppressing emotion. He knew there was a warm and loving person beneath her tough exterior, but it was usually reserved for others and never directed at him.

"I should take Dad's car back," she said, sidestepping the point he was trying to make about cooperation. "He'll be worried, and I have no cell phone for him to contact me on."

"Okay." He took his hand off her shoulder. "I'll take the lead and you follow. I'll come inside and explain to Leonardo what's happened." He picked up the lipstick tube from the roof of the car and pocketed it. "Then I'll go get you a spare cell phone from the fire station. You can borrow it until you replace yours. I'll file a report with Bear a little later."

"I hope you're right about being able to trust him, Cal."

He shrugged his shoulders. "With everything that's going on right now, I don't think we have a choice in the matter."

Olivia turned over the cell phone in her hands, thanking Cal for loaning it to her. It was a spare handset from the fire station, and it would serve her needs perfectly until she received the replacement she'd ordered in the mail. Leonardo sat with her and Cal in the kitchen, stone-faced and holding a large white envelope in his hands. On learning of the latest incident, Olivia's father hadn't been concerned about the dent to his bumper or his missed appointment, but he'd been near frantic about another attack on his daughter.

"I'm sorry I scared you, Dad," she said. "I know I made

a mistake." She didn't want to rehash the same points and make herself feel bad all over again, so she deftly changed the subject. "What's in the envelope?"

"It's for Cal," Leonardo replied, sliding it to him across the table. "It contains all the financial information about Moretti's he requested before the purchase contract is drawn up by the lawyers. It's been sent electronically, but I'm old-school so I like dealing with paper copies."

Cal took the envelope while Olivia watched intently. Inside that fat envelope was the accounting data she'd been asking her father to hand over for years. All she wanted was to understand why the café's profits were dwindling. And now Cal would get to see this information with a simple click of his fingers.

She reached for the envelope. "Could I just take a quick peek?"

"No, Olivia," her father said. "It's for Cal only."

The unfairness of being locked out of the data for the business she'd run—basically on her own, and very successfully—for the past several years caused Olivia to suddenly see red. And Cal was the obvious target for her anger.

"I know Moretti's Café inside out," she said, fixing her stare on him. "I know every nook and cranny of that place, every polished handle and every tiny crack in the floor tiles. Nobody is more qualified to manage Moretti's than I am." She took a deep breath. "And I mean nobody."

Cal looked at her. "Then stay," he said matter-of-factly. "Stay and work for me."

"You know I can't. We couldn't stand to work together."

"Why not?" he asked. "You and Rosalie could continue as always. I'd stay in the background. I know you have two other part-time staff, and they're welcome to stay too."

She thought about remaining in the job she loved with

her best friend by her side. No matter how attractive the prospect seemed, Cal would still be her boss. How could she keep all the pictures of her grandfather on the walls when the place belonged to a Mackenzie? It would feel like such a betrayal of his memory.

"I can't," she said, standing up. "You have no idea what you're asking."

She fled the room before the tears began to flow.

FIVE

Olivia and Rosalie did a little happy dance around the kitchen, holding each other's hands while twirling around. Olivia had received a telephone call from the Maple Valley Bank that morning, inviting her to an appointment at their office in the neighboring town of Granton in five days' time. After speaking to the bank manager, Olivia had immediately called Rosalie to give her the good news, and the two women now planned on creating a business plan together, detailing how Moretti's was a solid investment for the bank under her leadership. Olivia knew her father would never hand over the official financial figures, but she could use her own data, based on till receipts and invoices, to prove the café's excellent profits.

"You can't go to Granton by yourself, right?" Rosalie asked, typically focusing on the practical aspects. She'd always been the sensible one. "You gonna ask Conceited Cal to take you?"

Olivia nodded. "Actually, he's been way less conceited lately. He's been…" She stopped to consider the right word to choose. "Nice."

Rosalie made a face. "Nice Cal doesn't have the same ring to it, does it?" She sat on a chair at the table. "I wish I could drive you places and pull my weight. It's frustrating."

"Hey, you do plenty for me," Olivia said, sitting next to her. "You've been my rock for years. We have each other's back."

Rosalie had a mild form of epilepsy and didn't hold a driver's license, so her husband, Martin, acted as her personal taxi service whenever she needed to get somewhere outside of walking distance. Unfortunately, Rosalie's anti-seizure medication had caused her to experience fertility problems. Despite trying for two years, she had not conceived, and Rosalie had cried on Olivia's shoulder many times. The two friends leaned on each other heavily in times of crisis. Olivia didn't know what she'd have done without Rosalie's love and support over the years, but now somebody else was also becoming a surprising pillar of strength in her life. And that person was Cal.

Rosalie reached over and took Olivia's hand. "I'm glad you have Cal to help out. I know it must be strange being close to him, but from what I've seen, he's trying really hard. He called me yesterday to ask how you're holding up. He was worried about you after you got followed by a car on the mountain road."

Olivia raised her eyebrows. It felt a little intrusive for Cal and Rosalie to talk about her behind her back, but could she really get upset with him for worrying about her? She remembered how Cal had recently reminded her to try to put their rivalry behind them. She shouldn't be so quick to judge him harshly.

"What did you tell him?" she asked.

"I told him you'd secretly been in love with him ever since you shared that amazing kiss on prom night." Rosalie was smirking. "And you want to marry him and live happily ever after."

Olivia narrowed her eyes. "What did you really say?"

"I said you're doing just fine. You're the same old stubborn, determined Olivia you've always been."

Olivia tilted her head. "Why does that feel like an insult?"

"Because you're too stubborn to take it as a compliment," Rosalie said with a laugh.

"Did Cal mention anything about you working for him if he buys the café?" Olivia asked tentatively. "He talked about it yesterday, but I couldn't face it." She pressed the heels of her hands into her eyes, thinking of her cowardice. "I ran away."

"He told me my job is safe," Rosalie replied. "But I don't think I could stay at Moretti's if he became the boss. It would be weird, right? I mean, it's Cal. You've always considered him your arch nemesis." She raised one eyebrow. "Apart from that one time behind the drapes, of course."

Olivia smiled. Only Rosalie was allowed to tease her about the kiss.

"Do you really think it would be too strange working for Conceited Cal?" she said.

Rosalie wrinkled her brows. "I thought we'd renamed him Nice Cal?"

"How about Cautious Cal?" Olivia suggested. "Because he's treading carefully around us."

"Cute Cal?" Rosalie offered, bursting into laughter. "I know you think he's good-looking, especially in his uniform."

"Stop it," Olivia said, laughing along. "Don't you dare tell him that."

At that moment, Leonardo entered the kitchen, carrying a tray of breakfast dishes from Francesca's bedroom.

"What's gotten you girls in fits of giggles?" he asked, sliding the tray onto the counter.

"Just a silly joke," Olivia replied, wiping beneath her

eyes. "Listen, Dad, I have an appointment at Maple Valley Bank on Friday. I've applied for a loan to purchase Moretti's, so hopefully you won't have to sell to Cal."

She saw her father's shoulders stiffen and his face tighten. He didn't welcome this news.

"That's not a viable option, Olivia," he said. "You'd need some kind of collateral like a property to secure a business loan like that. I don't want you to be disappointed."

"I know it's a long shot," she said. "But I'll draw up a business plan and prove I'm a risk worth taking. The manager said he can offer some leeway in certain situations. I have to explore every avenue to protect Nonno's legacy."

Her father fell silent.

"What aren't you telling me, Dad?" she challenged. "Because it's obvious you're holding something back."

Leonardo glanced at Rosalie, who took the hint, rising from her chair and excusing herself from the room. She clearly sensed this was a private conversation.

"There's a running cost associated with the café that you're not aware of," Leonardo said as soon as they were alone. "You won't be able to afford to pay it."

"What cost? If I won't be able to afford it, then surely neither would Cal."

"This particular cost wouldn't be passed on to Cal," he said cryptically. "Because it's only inherited by the Morettis."

Olivia was confused. "What are you talking about? What does the cost relate to?"

"I can't tell you that. You'll just have to trust me. The café should be sold outside the family."

"No," she stated firmly, refusing to back down. For years, she'd deferred to her father about the café's business decisions, and look where it had left them. She wasn't going to just accept the loss of the café. Not without a much better explanation than her father had been willing to give her so far. "Stop treating me with kid gloves and tell me what's going on."

"I can't." Her father was raising his voice in response to her. "I made a promise."

"A promise to who?"

"To your grandfather. I inherited the running cost from him, and I refuse to pass the burden along to you. It must end here and now. The sale contract will be signed in two weeks, and that's final."

Leonardo walked from the room, leaving his daughter with a bunch of unanswered questions. What exactly didn't she know? And more importantly, how would she uncover the secret?

Cal checked that Olivia wasn't within earshot before sitting at the kitchen table in the Moretti family home. The forecast heavy rainfall hadn't yet arrived, so he'd been afforded a little respite in his duties. The forest landslide was holding firm, and the reservoir dam wasn't currently in danger of breaching. As Cal had been working way more hours than his colleagues recently, he'd been given flexibility in when he could take time off, and he'd allocated an hour that morning to discuss a sensitive matter with Leonardo.

"I appreciate all you've done to take care of Olivia and the townsfolk," Leonardo said, placing a mug of coffee in front of him. "I hope we've seen the worst of the weather."

Cal shook his head. "Don't get your hopes up. We're bracing for more serious rainfall soon." He looked toward the door. "Where's Olivia?"

"She's holed up in the den with Rosalie working on a business plan for her bank appointment on Friday," Leonardo replied. "She's applied for a loan to purchase Moretti's, but I think it's a bad idea. I hope she changes her mind."

Cal knew all about the appointment in Granton. Olivia had already asked him to drive her there and back, and he'd readily agreed. He was, however, not hopeful of her achieving her goal. He'd been required to jump through a lot of hoops when applying for a business loan. His apartment had been used as collateral, and his parents had agreed to act as guarantors. Olivia had no such assets to draw on.

"You think it's a bad idea?" He was surprised at Leonardo's attitude. "You'd rather the café was sold to a non-family member?"

"Yes, I would. It's a…complicated matter to do with finances. I can't discuss it with you."

"Actually," Cal said, shifting in his seat awkwardly. "That's what I'm here to discuss. There's a question I need to ask about the data you supplied."

Leonardo nodded, as if he'd been expecting this. "Go ahead."

"The money coming into the café is healthy," he said. "After the mortgage, salaries and utilities are paid, you should have plenty of profit, but it's all being transferred out each month. In fact, in some months, the amount taken out has left you without enough to cover your expenses—which is how you ended up falling behind on your mortgage. I wondered if you could shed some light on what's going on."

Leonardo fidgeted with the handle on his mug and took a few seconds to reply.

"I need the café's profits to service a large payment each month," he said. "It's nothing for you to worry about because it's a personal matter."

"You're making personal payments from a business account?"

Leonardo squirmed, looking highly uncomfortable. "I own the business—the profits are mine to do with as I see fit. But the debt belongs to the Moretti family. It's not tied to the café itself."

"So I won't need to make the same payment?"

"No," Leonardo said firmly. "Like I said, it's a personal matter. Your lawyer will be able to highlight all the expenses of the café, and this particular one isn't part of them."

This set Cal's mind at rest. His lawyer had already assured him there were no hidden costs associated with the purchase, but he'd been worried about the disappearance of the café's monthly profits. But now that he knew the money wasn't part of a business expense, he was concerned about what personal burdens might be weighing on Leonardo.

The sixty-five-year-old was looking tired and unshaven, with rings beneath his eyes. What was this personal debt he had to pay? Did he have gambling problems? Or maybe, like his father, he'd had affairs? The payments could be child support. Cal shook his head and reminded himself not to speculate. It was none of his business. The most he could do would be to offer to listen, if Leonardo felt like sharing.

"Are you okay?" Cal asked. "Is there anything you want to talk about?"

Cal knew people's situations weren't always simple. Money problems were common enough for all kinds of reasons, and Leonardo might not have anybody to turn to.

"I'm fine," he replied with a weak smile. "I can manage my own problems, but I worry about Olivia. She's taking the loss of the café very hard, and I think it's why she's throwing herself so strongly into this investigation. She wants to protect her grandfather's legacy—his café—as well as his reputation. She's agitating some local people, especially men who have secrets to hide." He rubbed his bristly chin. "Somebody is upset enough to try to hurt her." He stopped for a moment as his lip wobbled. "She's my sweet daughter and I love her more than she knows. All I want to do is protect her."

Cal patted Leonardo's hand reassuringly. "I want to protect her too. Olivia and I have never been close, but I've always secretly admired her. And recently, I've gotten to know her a lot better, and found that there's a lot about her to like."

Leonardo smiled. "She's not always easy to get close to," he said. "But once she lets you in, she's easy to love, I can promise you that."

"I'm sure she is." Cal had always imagined himself loving a woman like Olivia—strong and capable with a fiercely caring instinct. "But I don't think Olivia and I will ever go there."

Leonardo regarded him for a long time before speaking.

"My father did a lot of damage to the relationships between the Mackenzies and the Morettis," he said, finally. "He encouraged us to view your family with hostility. Since he's been gone, I've repaired a lot of that damage with your folks, but Olivia is still learning how to let go of the past. I've often wondered if you two would've been friends if it hadn't been for her grandfather's influence. You seem good together."

Cal's color rose. Perhaps Leonardo was right.

"Who's good together?"

Olivia appeared in the doorway. She was wearing comfortable sweats, and her hair was tied up in a ponytail right on the top of her head, so her curls cascaded across her shoulders like a soft veil. She looked more beautiful than ever, and Cal found himself surprisingly tongue-tied.

"Um…it doesn't matter," he said, rising to stand. "I gotta get back to work. Thanks for the chat, Leonardo."

"I'll walk you to the door," Olivia said, following him out into the hallway. "I have a favor to ask."

He stopped in the hallway. "Sure."

"I'd like to go visit Dennis Clark," she said in a whisper. "Can you come with me?"

Dennis was the owner of a wholesale grocery store on the outskirts of town. Now in his late fifties, he'd been managing the business for about thirty-five years.

"If you need provisions, I can get them for you," he said. "Just make a list."

"I need to see Dennis in person," she hissed, her dark brown eyes settled intently on his. "About a private matter. He's agreed to see me at seven o'clock on Wednesday evening."

Realization dawned. "Oh, right. It's part of your investigation."

"Yes."

Leonardo's words about Olivia agitating local people still rang in his ears.

"Are you sure you want to do this?" he asked. "It might cause more harm than good."

"I can find somebody else to go with me if you object," she said, opening the door for him to leave. "It's not a problem."

"Of course I'll take you," he said. "I just want you to think about the consequences of what you're doing."

"Consequences?" she questioned. "Why do I feel like I'm in the school principal's office?"

"I'm not scolding you. Or judging you. I'm giving you friendly advice."

"Thanks, Cal," she said as he stepped outside. "I'll take it under advisement."

He turned around to face her, only to find she'd already

shut the door before he'd said goodbye. He shook his head and smiled. Leonardo was right about Olivia not making it easy to get close to her. Yet Cal suspected her father was absolutely correct about her being easy to love.

Olivia had been skirting round her father all afternoon. Leonardo was showing signs of anxiety. He kept mislaying things and muttering angrily to himself while trying to find them. Olivia had tried to stay out of his way, because she didn't want to run the risk of challenging him about the brief conversation they'd had that morning. She was still bristling at the way her father had shut her down, refusing to divulge the mysterious running cost attached to the café. He was treating her like a child, and Cal's involvement in business matters only made her feel worse. She felt as though Cal was invading her space, pushing her out and taking her place. He wasn't acting maliciously but her identity was so tied up in the café that the thought of someone else taking her place hurt deeply.

"Olivia!" her father was calling up the stairs. "You have visitors."

She grabbed her cell and made her way downstairs, surprised to see Bear and Cal sitting at the kitchen table. She could hear the drone of the television in the living room as her grandmother watched an old musical. Francesca couldn't follow a plot these days, so musicals were her favorite movies. Even when she couldn't keep track of the story, she could still enjoy the musical numbers.

"I'll go sit with my mother," Leonardo said, leaving the kitchen and closing the door.

"Hi, Olivia," Bear said. "I'm here to take a statement about the car that pursued you on the mountain road. Cal showed me the pictures of the message left on your windshield in lipstick." He reached into his pocket and pulled out a small black tube, which he placed on the table. "Cal had the presence of mind to retrieve it from the scene."

Olivia felt a fleeting moment of irritation at another conversation about her taking place behind her back, but let it pass. Cal had told her he'd be filing a report, so it wasn't really a surprise. And while she still felt Bear was holding some things back, she accepted Cal was right. If she was going to see the perpetrator brought to justice, she had to cooperate with the authorities.

"Bear contacted the lipstick manufacturer," Cal said. "This shade was discontinued twenty-seven years ago. That means it might've belonged to Sadie. It's a good lead to follow."

"That's great," she said, feeling a much-needed injection of hope. "It might even lead us all the way to the car owner." She went to the kitchen counter and filled the percolator with water. "I'll make some coffee." She pointed at Cal. "Black, no sugar, right?"

He smiled and winked. "You know I'm sweet enough already."

Olivia laughed. "Are you sure about that? I think you like the bitterness."

He chuckled. "I should know better than to verbally spar with you. You always have the upper hand with words."

"Do you remember the time we argued in the lunch line at school in eighth grade?" she asked while placing coffee in the machine. "I said you were as useful as a chocolate fireguard, and you said if insults were a spice, that one would be flour. That was a great comeback."

Cal threw back his head and guffawed. "Yeah, I remember it well, but good comebacks didn't happen often for me."

"I quietly admired you for that one," she said. "Although I never told you."

"Hold up a second," Bear said, raising his hands in the air. "What's going on here? Are you two friends now? You seem to be getting along pretty well."

Olivia busied herself with making coffee to avoid her blush being seen. She'd been ignoring her shifting feelings for Cal and had hoped nobody else would see it. But now Bear had commented on their growing closeness, and she wanted to shut down the scrutiny immediately.

"Let's not get ahead of ourselves, Bear," she said. "Cal and I will probably be fighting again by tomorrow."

Cal stood at the edge of the Redwood Reservoir with his hands on his hips, surveying the huge and glistening body of water in front of him. The lake had swelled considerably during the last seven days but was still within the safety limit due to the effective use of spillways. However, a fine drizzle had begun to fall that afternoon and was forecast to turn heavier overnight. That would put additional pressure on the embankment dam, which was made of a mixture of soil and rock. The dam had been modified several times in recent years, making it longer and higher, but not making it stronger, despite Cal filing numerous complaints with the water system operator, pointing out that the dam showed serious cracking in times of heavy rain. A dam failure would have catastrophic consequences for the western side of Abbeywood, where the Redwood Estates housing complex was located. This cluster of one hundred houses would be directly in the path of any escaping water.

He closed his eyes and bowed his head for a few seconds, asking for wisdom and guidance. The dam owners still hadn't allocated a team to oversee the problem, and the mayor had asked Cal to take responsibility for monitoring this potential hazard. The decision over whether or not to evacuate weighed heavily on Cal's mind. Local churches and community organizations had already opened their doors to assist residents whose homes were flooded, but nobody wanted to sleep on a camping bed in a noisy dormitory unless it was necessary.

He pulled his camera from his pocket to take photographs of the cracks in the dam so he could email them to the water operator later that day. He had a long list of duties to perform before returning to his office at the fire station. He needed to go check on the landslide, visit North Bridge to assess the situation there and make a brief stop at Main Street to ensure no properties were in danger of collapse. He'd already sent his team to the town center to shore up the flood defenses and monitor the water levels. Their hourly updates were reassuring, indicating no emergency issues so far.

Cal made his way to his truck as Olivia's face crept into his thoughts. He'd been unable to get her off his mind recently, and he didn't know what to do about it. He frequently got distracted when he saw something that reminded him of her, like the evening primroses growing on the hillsides. She loved to pick these flowers and place them in little vases on the tables in Moretti's. She also liked to watch sunrises over the river when she opened the café at dawn. While making his way home at the end of his night shifts, he sometimes saw her standing at the riverside wall on Main Street with her face turned skyward so that the first rays of sunlight bathed her face. He always wanted to know what she was thinking at these moments. He hadn't realized it at the time, but he'd been developing feelings for her that were now making themselves known.

He was beginning to see Olivia in a new light and reassess everything he thought he knew about her. They weren't natural enemies. He was sure of it. When they first met in elementary school, while his parents were still working on opening their café and had not yet become competitors with Moretti's, she often shared her sweet Italian treats from her lunch box. Cal could still taste the wonderful way the pastry melted in his mouth. But Mario put a stop to that as soon as Mackenzie's opened.

In fact, Mario always seemed to intervene whenever he and Olivia got too close. When Olivia was ten years old, she'd let Cal borrow her bike, but Mario demanded it back when he saw Cal riding it outside his home. At twelve, Olivia passed Cal a tissue in church when he had a fit of sneezes, only for Mario to scold her for it. At thirteen, she surreptitiously passed Cal a five-dollar bill in a convenience store when he realized at the cash register that he'd forgotten his money. But then she wouldn't let him get close enough to her to pay her back, too worried that someone would report back to her grandfather that they'd been seen talking.

Each of those small acts of kindness had been lost in among Cal and Olivia's subsequent arguments and animosity, but they were now coming to the forefront of his mind. She wasn't a hostile person inside. Mario had tried to mold her to be that way, but it only went as far as the surface. Now that she'd put some of her animosity to rest, Cal was getting a chance to see more of the loving woman who was emerging from Mario's shadow.

"Oh boy," he said, rubbing his nape. "What's happening to me? I'm losing my focus."

As he reached his truck and sat inside, he realized that his focus was exactly where it wanted to be. Olivia was becoming ever more special to him, and it was a worrying development. She would never feel the same way. He would need to stop these stupid daydreams and learn to toughen up.

Olivia couldn't sleep. She was too excited about the prospect of being able to purchase Moretti's for herself. Added to her excitement were nerves about meeting Dennis the following day. Would he be friendly? Or would he be hostile like Randy? She just didn't know. Maybe she'd discover that he was the one behind the attacks on her.

Bear had promised to leave no stone unturned in his effort to locate the black car that had pursued her, and despite his relationship with Sadie, Olivia had made the decision to trust him. Besides, it would be hypocritical of her to judge Bear too harshly when that's exactly what the folks of Abbeywood were doing to her grandfather. Nobody in the town gave Mario a chance. From the moment Sadie's body was found, he'd been judged guilty without so much as a second's thought.

Pouring hot water into her mug, she inhaled the sweet smell of her fruit tea rising with the steam. The clock on the wall had just passed midnight and the whole house was silent and dark. The only sound she could hear was the gentle patter of drops on the kitchen window. The rain was growing heavier as the night wore on, and this would surely lead to rising floods. She hoped Moretti's wouldn't be too badly damaged. If things went her way, she'd be cleaning up and reopening as soon as possible.

A noise caught her attention. In the backyard, a lawn chair scraped on the patio, as if it had been knocked or jolted. Olivia walked to the window with her mug in hand and peered into the blackness of night. Sometimes foxes or deer ventured into the yard seeking food, but she couldn't see any signs of wildlife. Pulling down the blind, she told herself there was nothing to worry about. The attacks only came when she was alone and in a position that made it easy for her attacker to strike. But here at home, she was with her dad. Not to mention, all the doors and windows were securely locked, and the security lights would alert her to anybody approaching the house.

Another noise sounded outside, and her body gave a start, spilling hot tea onto her hand. She put down her mug on the counter and ran her hand under cold water. She could hear footsteps on the backyard path, slow and dragging. She switched off the faucet and held her hand in a dry dishcloth, clutching it to her chest, where her heart pounded like a hammer. The footsteps suddenly ceased. Could this be a heavy-footed animal? She didn't want to believe it was her attacker—wanted to feel that her home was still safe, even if nowhere else was—but she should check from a higher vantage point to be sure of who or what was out there.

Still holding the cloth around her sore hand, she headed upstairs to her bedroom, which overlooked the backyard. She thought about calling Cal, just to be safe, but it wasn't right to drag him out of bed at this time of night just because she was spooked. In truth, she'd rather not be required to call him at all. She was becoming way too reliant on him, and she hated to admit that butterflies sometimes erupted in her belly when he entered a room. He made her smile even when she was determined to frown. These unwelcome feelings of attraction had snuck up on her without warning, and she intended on suppressing them. Before the flooding occurred, she'd never even considered Cal to be a friend. Now she looked forward to seeing him. She was obviously lonely and not thinking straight.

Parting the drapes in her room, Olivia scanned the yard

below. In the gloom, she saw the outline of the summer-
house, the large beech trees and the patio furniture. The
rain fell steadily over all of it, giving the scene a slick and
glossy appearance. Nobody appeared to be there.

Movement caught her eye. A shadowy outline was lurk-
ing beneath one of the trees, hunched over, as if protecting himself against the elements. Olivia narrowed her eyes
while her breath quickened. She didn't know if she could
trust her eyesight in the dim light. Was this a man's outline or an animal?

Her question was quickly answered when the man stepped
out of the cover of the tree and began walking purposefully
toward the house. The security light activated, illuminating
him in a bright glow. The man was wearing a black poncho
that she associated with fishermen. The hood was pulled
firmly over his head, so she could see no part of his face at
all. He stood on the edge of the path, right by the back door,
as the rain snaked down his waterproof cape and pants. In
his right hand she saw an object. It didn't look like a gun,
but she thought it might be a knife. Whatever it was, she felt
certain it was a weapon of some kind.

Now Olivia knew she must call Cal. Fumbling with her
cell phone on the nightstand, her hand shook as she found
his number and pressed the call button. She'd expected
him to be groggy on answering but he wasn't. He was instantly alert.

"Olivia," he said. "It's late. Has something happened?"

"An intruder is here. He's out in the yard and he's holding something in his hand."

Cal sprang into action.

"Listen to me carefully," he said. "Go wake your dad
and take him into your grandmother's room. Barricade the
door and stay there until help arrives. I'll call the police

right away, but I'll probably arrive before they do. Don't answer the door for anybody but me or law enforcement."

"My dad has a gun. Should I take it with us?"

"Yes, but only use it if you really need to. I'm heading out the door as I speak. I'll be with you in a few minutes. Don't hang up. Go wake your dad right now but keep me on speaker."

"Okay."

She activated the speaker mode on the cell and slipped it into the pocket of her robe, hearing Cal place an emergency call on his truck radio. Then she went into her father's room and shook him awake. He was confused and sleepy, reaching for his glasses on the nightstand before sitting up in bed.

"There's an intruder outside," she said quickly. "Get your gun and let's go into Nonna's room. Cal's on his way, and he's called the police already."

"What?" Her father didn't seem able to take in her words. "Are you sure?"

"Yes," she said. "Come see for yourself."

She parted the drapes across the window, half expecting the man to have vanished. But he was still there, bathed in the bright glow of the security light. She felt a little relief at the sight of him. At least she knew where he was.

Then, slowly and with deliberate movements, he drew back his right arm. That's when she identified the object in his hand as a brick. And she knew exactly where it would be heading. In the next moment, there was an almighty crash from below, as the kitchen window smashed into hundreds of tiny pieces.

SIX

Cal stood well away from the glass that littered the kitchen floor. The pieces fanned out in all directions, ranging from large, pointed shards to tiny, almost invisible fragments. Olivia stood next to him in her pajamas, robe and slippers, clutching a cup of fruit tea to her chest. The liquid had gone cold long ago, but she seemed unable to put down the mug, and was apparently using it as a buffer between her and the world. By the time Cal arrived at the house, the intruder had fled into the night, leaving behind nothing but a whole lot of mess.

As the clock approached seven in the morning, Bear was photographing the scene, wearing a sweat suit that he must've thrown on as soon as he woke up and heard the news. It was a job Bear could've delegated to one of his deputies, but the sheriff must have insisted on attending himself. He seemed determined to prove to Olivia that he was trustworthy. She was watching him step carefully around the broken glass, taking numerous photographs. Finally, he put down his camera on the table, next to the brick that had been hurled with malice into the Morettis' lives.

"Somebody sure wants to send you a message," Bear said, holding up the piece of paper that had been secured around the brick with a rubber band. "This is pretty clear, huh?"

Cal saw Olivia flinch as she once again read the words written in bold black marker: *ARE YOU SCARED YET?* The note was obviously aimed at Olivia, but Cal knew it would take more than a broken window to deter her from her investigation. She was nothing if not determined.

"I'll ask forensics to dust this for prints," Bear said, sliding the note into a plastic bag and sealing it. "But this guy is probably smart enough to wear gloves." He looked at Olivia. "It would be a good idea to install two security cameras around the exterior of the house, at the front and back. Maybe you could get it done at the same time you fix the window."

Cal held up a hand. "It's already organized, Bear."

Cal had taken a call from Pastor Brian just a few minutes ago, during which the pastor had insisted on paying for any repairs and security upgrades to the Morettis' home. Abbeywood Church had a community fund, which was administered by the pastor to help church members in crisis. Brian said that he knew that money was tight for Morettis, and he wanted to make their house safe and secure without delay. Hence, the church had arranged for a glazier and a camera installer to visit later in the day. In the meantime, Cal had secured plywood over the gaping hole to keep out the wind and rain.

"Take a seat, guys," Bear said, pulling out a couple of chairs from beneath the table. "I have some news on the car that pursued Olivia recently." He looked toward her. "Do you want your dad to be part of this conversation?"

She quickly shook her head. "He's settling Nonna upstairs. She's agitated by what's happened."

Cal took the cold mug from Olivia's grip and set it on

the counter. He refilled it with hot water from the kettle before adding a peppermint tea bag. Then he sat next to her at the table and slid the mug back into her hands. She was quiet and sad, in stark contrast to her upbeat attitude from the previous day. Her mood had deflated like an old party balloon.

"I've identified the black car that followed you," Bear said. "The logging company was very quick to send the footage from their security camera. Leonardo's car and the black car appear on the footage for only a few seconds, but it was enough to establish a make and model of the vehicle."

Olivia instantly perked up. "Do you have a license plate?"

"The car had no plates attached, but we know it's a Pontiac Firebird. It's a third-generation model, probably around thirty-five to forty years old. It has a distinctive paint job with two white stripes on the hood, so I can say with a fair amount of confidence that I've never seen it around Abbeywood before. Have either of you?"

Both Olivia and Cal shook their heads.

"The car is old, just like the lipstick," Olivia said. "Do you think it could have been Sadie's vehicle?"

Bear thought long and hard, closing his eyes to cast his mind back. "Sadie drove a beat-up blue Volkswagen. She was only a bartender, so I don't think she could afford a Firebird. The lipstick might've been hers though. It's the color she used to wear. Maybe she was involved with the guy who owns the car, and she left some makeup in his glove box." He sighed. "It's going to be a challenge to trace the Firebird's history. Most car dealerships don't keep records going that far back, and I have no idea where it was purchased anyway. All I can do is put out an alert to all law enforcement agencies to be on the lookout for it. Hopefully, someone with a badge will spot it and pull it over."

"You could ask Randy if Sadie owned a Firebird," Olivia suggested. "He's bound to know, right?"

Bear shot her a disapproving look. "Absolutely not. Randy has made it clear that he doesn't want to be contacted. I'd need to have a very good reason for knocking on his door."

"Both Randy and Bobby fit the body type of the intruder," Olivia said. "That's a reason to question them."

"The description you provided matches about forty percent of the men in Abbeywood," Bear replied. "We need something more to identify him."

"Olivia's stalker isn't Randy or Bobby." These words came from Leonardo, who was standing in the doorway, having been eavesdropping on their conversation. "I called Randy last night to ask what he knows about these attacks, and he assured me that neither he nor his son is responsible."

Bear let out a groan. "Seriously, Leonardo? I already gave your daughter a warning for harassing the Billinghams and now you're doing the same thing."

"I just needed to be certain it wasn't them," Leonardo said, coming into the room, in his pajamas and slippers. "The whole town believes my father killed Randy's wife. I thought they might be out for revenge."

Bear stood up and held his palms in the air with splayed fingers. "Leave the investigating to the professionals. If you don't have a badge, don't go bothering people." He looked at the three faces in the room. "Got it?"

Cal exchanged a knowing glance with Olivia. Tomorrow evening, they would be paying a visit to Dennis Clark, where Olivia would ask him what he knew about Sadie's disappearance and murder. Cal didn't see anything wrong with it, as Dennis had agreed to the meeting, but Bear would see things differently.

Olivia held Cal's gaze, silently willing him not to reveal their clandestine meeting with the local store owner. Try as he might, he couldn't help but feel a sense of pleasure at sharing a secret with her, as if this gave them a special connection. These feelings of strong attachment were new and unfamiliar. He couldn't work out if he simply wanted to protect a vulnerable woman or if his romantic notions went deeper. Either way, Bear would be unlikely to give Cal any leeway in assisting Olivia's questioning of Dennis. Hence, he thought it best not to mention it.

"Got it, Bear," he said. "I'll keep Olivia out of trouble."

Abbeywood was super dark the following night. No moonlight could penetrate the thick cloud, and steady rainfall fell from an inky sky. Olivia was glad Cal was driving. He knew where the puddles were deepest and what roads to avoid. She'd been pleased and surprised that he'd agreed to accompany her to see Dennis, despite Bear's warnings. They still had their differences, but for the most part, Cal supported her in her choices. They even joked and laughed together these days, which had been the most surprising development in their relationship. Cal was behaving in a sweet and generous way. It wasn't how things usually played out between them, and it unsettled her a little. The dynamic between them had shifted considerably.

"Here we are," Cal said, pulling into the parking lot of Clark's Wholesale Foods. "Right on time."

Olivia could see Dennis through the store's glass frontage. He was standing behind the counter but on seeing them exit Cal's truck, he came out the door, still wearing his store-branded apron. He seemed wary and looked up and down the road, checking the surroundings.

"Randy says I shouldn't be talking to you," he said. "He reckons you're a troublemaker."

Olivia's stomach dropped. She knew Bobby and Dennis were good friends, so she'd been worried about the Billinghams sabotaging her meeting.

"Making trouble is not my intention at all," she protested. "I just want to get to the truth. You have nothing to hide, right?"

Dennis rubbed his nape, as if uncomfortable. His face was round and ruddy, and he wore a beanie hat pulled low over his ears.

"Randy admitted to me that he told you about my relationship with Sadie," he said. "He shouldn't have done it and he's sorry about it now. Bobby and I have been friends since high school, and when I was twenty-two, I made a stupid mistake by having a fling with his stepmom. Randy knew about it, but Bobby never found out. Randy and I have kept it a secret until now, so I'd appreciate this information remaining private."

"I have no plans to expose your affair, Mr. Clark," she said, pulling the hood of her raincoat over her head. "Do you think we could get out of the rain while we talk?"

Dennis shook his head. "Just ask me what you want to know, and you can be on your way."

This wasn't the kind of meeting Olivia had had in mind. She'd hoped for a civil discussion indoors, but if a cold and wet conversation was the only thing on offer, she'd have to take it.

"Did Sadie ever mention my grandfather while you two were together?"

"All the time," Dennis replied. "She was in love with him, but he wouldn't leave his wife, which upset her a lot. She went out looking for young men to numb the pain or maybe to make him jealous. I'm not sure which. I was brain-less enough to take what was on offer, but I quickly realized I was being an idiot. I had a girlfriend, and she didn't de-serve to be cheated on. I ended things with Sadie and pro-posed to my girlfriend a little while after. We've now been married thirty-two years, and I don't want my wife know-ing what happened before we tied the knot. Even though it was a long time ago, she'd still take it hard. Infidelity is a red line for her."

"When you ended your relationship with Sadie, how did she take it?" Olivia asked. "Was she upset?"

Dennis laughed scornfully. "Sadie only had eyes for Mario Moretti. Go ask Gina from the Hangout Bar where Sadie worked. Gina knew Sadie better than anybody." He checked his watch. "It closes at ten so you could go right now."

Olivia had never been to the Hangout Bar. It was on the outskirts of town, and she'd heard it was kind of sleazy, at-tracting hardened drinkers who didn't always observe DUI laws. She looked at Cal and he gave her a tiny nod, indicat-ing his agreement, and she steeled herself to ask Dennis one last question before leaving.

"Did you have access to Moretti's Café at the time of Sadie's murder?"

Dennis stood up straight. "What exactly are you saying? Are you accusing me of putting her there?"

"Not at all," she said calmly. "I'm just trying to work out who might've had keys to the building."

"Randy was right to warn me about you," he said, as the mood grew hostile. "You're so desperate to get your grandfa-ther off the hook, you'll blame an innocent man for murder."

Cal placed an arm around Olivia's shoulders, and she was thankful for the reminder that he was there to support her.

"Olivia isn't blaming you, Dennis," he said. "You don't have to provide an answer if you don't want to, but it's best to be honest about it, rather than evade the question."

"Cal's right," she chimed in. "I'm not judging you. We all make mistakes, including me. *Especially* me."

"I used to supply Moretti's with all kinds of food," Dennis said. "So of course I had access to the café. My store had only just started out in those days, and Moretti's was a big fish to land. I went the extra mile to make early-morning deliveries twice a week, so Mario gave me a key to put the items in the cellar before he arrived."

"Did anybody else know where you kept the key?" Olivia asked. "Did you ever notice it go missing?"

Dennis shook his head. "No to both questions. You gotta face the facts, Miss Moretti. Your grandfather killed his mistress and buried her body in his cellar. He got himself a new food supplier after Sadie vanished, and he asked me to return the key. In hindsight, it's obvious Mario didn't want me spotting any changes to the wall in the cellar. He was covering his tracks."

"You're making assumptions," she said, trying to retain her cool. "We don't know what happened."

He threw his arms up in the air. "Of course we know what happened. Mario Moretti was an adulterer and a murderer."

"You're no saint yourself, Mr. Clark," she shot back, stung by his cruel words. "Maybe you should look in the mirror."

"Get off my parking lot!" he said, raising his voice. "I think we're done here."

Cal took her firmly by the shoulder and steered her toward his truck.

"Let's go," he said. "Before somebody says something they really regret."

"You agree with Dennis, don't you, Cal?" she said, climbing into the passenger seat. "You think my grandfather was an adulterer and a murder."

"It doesn't matter what I think," he said with a shrug. "It matters what *you* think."

As he walked around to the driver's side, Olivia closed her eyes and breathed deeply. It definitely mattered to her what Cal thought. It mattered a lot. And she wished it didn't. How had he snuck into her life like this? He was no longer simply the person trying to purchase her family's café. He had become someone whose opinion she valued and whose advice she craved.

And that just wouldn't do at all.

The Hangout Bar was as seedy as Olivia imagined. The dingy lighting failed to hide the stains on the pool tables or the broken bar stools, which were held together with silver tape. The neon signs behind the bar cast a pale glow of red, blue and yellow across the place, but rather than looking festive, it only added to the depressing atmosphere. Olivia figured it might look different when the bar was full of people, but at that moment it was empty, with just one lonely bartender waiting to take orders. Apparently, the local flooding had kept the regulars away, and the bar's owners were considering closing until the waters receded. But in the meantime, Gina continued to work her daily shifts, passing the time by watching television behind the bar or scrolling through her phone.

Gina looked to be in her mid-fifties, with a hairstyle that hadn't been updated since the eighties. She wore a sequined shirt and blue jeans, with stiletto-heeled boots. She greeted Olivia and Cal warmly, telling them about the shortage of customers and asking them what they wanted to drink. It was then that Olivia explained the reason for their visit, and Gina opened up instantly, gushing about her former coworker's fun and friendly nature.

"It was awful what happened to Sadie," she said. "All this time, I thought she was living her best life in New York, but she was buried in a basement in Abbeywood." She bowed her head. "She didn't deserve that."

"Did you know she was having an affair with my grandfather?" Olivia asked. "Mario Moretti."

"Oh, sure I did, honey. She adored Mario. Randy had never been a good husband to Sadie, and she was looking for a way out of her marriage when they started their affair. Mario was fifteen years older than her, and he was financially secure. She thought he'd take care of her. But the more time she spent with him, the harder she fell for him."

"It sounds like you knew her well," Cal said. "What else can you tell us about her?"

"Sadie grew up in foster homes in Concord," Gina replied. "She experienced a lot of bad stuff that she didn't like to talk about. By the time she aged out of the system at eighteen, she was carrying a lot of emotional baggage and was desperate for love. Randy met her in a club where she worked, and he showered her with love and attention. She reckons he was looking for a replacement mother for his baby son, Bobby, after his birth mother walked out on him. Sadie married Randy just after she turned twenty and she spent the next twenty years under his thumb. He was mean, controlling—he got her hooked on drugs and used them to keep her in line. She said the only good thing to come out of her marriage was Bobby. Even though he wasn't her biological son, she loved him deeply." Gina shook her head sadly. "Sadie couldn't have kids, you see, so Bobby was the closest she got to having a child of her own. When he turned twenty-one, Sadie figured he was strong enough to cope without her, and she wanted to divorce Randy."

"Did you think it was strange for her to abandon Bobby when she disappeared?" Olivia asked. "Did that sound like something she would do?"

Gina shrugged. "I thought it was weird, but Sadie's head was messed up after Mario kept stringing her along. She'd convinced herself they were gonna get married and go on honeymoon to Sicily. It was obvious to me that Mario would never leave his wife, but Sadie wouldn't accept it. She refused to believe he was a liar. He was using her."

Olivia stared into her glass of Coca-Cola. None of this sounded like the Nonno she remembered—but she was coming to accept that she'd only ever seen one side of him. She knew he'd often been difficult, and after all she'd been told, she couldn't deny he was a cheater, but she assumed he was a good man beneath these human flaws. Gina's version of Mario was a lot different, and much less forgivable. No matter who killed Sadie, she'd been a victim of cruelty for a long time before her death, and it seemed like Mario had been part of that. Cal, sensing her difficulty, took over the questioning.

"Do you remember what happened around the time Sadie disappeared?" he asked. "Anything at all?"

"I'll tell you the same thing I told Bear when he came to ask me the same question," she said. "Mario killed Sadie. I'm sure of it."

Olivia looked up sharply. "How?"

Gina wrung her index finger in her hand. "Are you sure you want to hear this, honey?"

"Speak honestly," she replied. "I can handle it."

Gina took a deep breath. "I was working a shift with Sadie on the night she vanished. She was frustrated because she'd had another fight with Mario about his refusal to leave his wife. She helped herself to a few drinks from behind the bar and got a little worked up. Then she called him on the phone. She told him she planned to show up at his house after her shift to tell his wife everything. Just as we were preparing to close for the night, Mario tore into the parking lot and stormed into the bar. He was angry, and they had a huge argument. Mario called her some horrible names, and she cussed him out. Sadie asked me to leave so she could talk to him in private. I went home and when I came back to the bar the following day, I found a letter from her, saying she'd had enough of the situation and was heading to New York to start afresh."

"And you believed it?" Cal asked in apparent disbelief.

"Sure I did," Gina said. "Whenever Sadie and Mario got in a fight, she'd talk about running away to the city and leaving all her problems behind. Skipping town in the middle of the night was exactly the kind of thing I'd expect from her. I was actually proud of her for getting out—for having the guts to walk away from a bad marriage and an even worse affair. But I never expected her to cut contact with Bobby. That was a surprise. Poor Bobby spent thirty years thinking his stepmother left him." Gina's eyes welled up, but her voice turned harsh. "I wish I'd reported her bust-up with Mario to the police. Her body might've been found earlier, and Bobby would've gotten some closure much sooner. Mario should've paid the price for what he did. He got to grow old and die peacefully in his sleep. Meanwhile, Sadie was buried behind a brick wall in a cold cellar. Justice wasn't served."

Olivia stood abruptly. This was too tough to hear, and she wished she'd listened to the warning Gina had given her.

She'd convinced herself her grandfather was innocent of murder, but she couldn't hold on to that certainty anymore.

"I need some air," she said, stumbling from her stool. "Thank you, Gina."

Olivia burst through the exit door and stood with her face upturned, allowing the rain to mingle with her tears. In no time at all, the raindrops were soaking her hair and trickling onto her scalp. Normally she avoided the rain, due to the crimping effect it had on her curls, but in that moment, she didn't care what she looked like. She didn't care if Cal saw her with mascara down her face and hair frizzed up like wire wool.

"It's okay," he said, appearing in front of her. "I know it hurts."

He gathered her into his arms and uttered more soothing words. If she'd been planning on putting some distance between them, she was failing miserably. But at that moment, she simply didn't have the energy to resist.

Cal hugged Olivia tightly. She was obviously struggling to process the story she'd just heard from Gina. Sadie's last known movements did nothing to exonerate Mario. They only strengthened the case against him. Sadie had been threatening to tell Francesca about the affair, and it was very likely that Mario killed her in anger. It seemed like a straightforward case.

"I wish I'd never started this investigation," Olivia said. "Somebody warned me to let the dead sleep and I'm beginning to see their point."

"It's okay to want to know the whole truth," Cal said. "But sometimes we can't accept it until we're ready."

"I'm not ready to accept my grandfather is a killer," she said. "There must be something I'm missing." She pushed against him and took a step back. "What am I missing, Cal? Who else came here after Gina left the bar on the night Nonno and Sadie argued? Somebody else must've been here."

"Nobody else was here," he said gently. "It was just Mario and Sadie."

She balled her hands into fists and leaned forward, as if doubled over in physical pain.

"That can't be true," she said with a cry. "It was the night Sadie died, so she must've had contact with someone else after my grandfather left her alive and well. Nonno probably had no idea that Sadie was in danger." She snapped her fingers, remembering her earlier conversation with Dennis. "Dennis had a key to the café, right? Sadie might've called him to give her a ride home, and they could've gotten into a fight after he arrived. They might've..." She trailed off. "I don't know, but there are still other possibilities." She covered her face with her hands as if trying to physically hide from the truth. "Nonno didn't kill Sadie, did he, Cal? Tell me he didn't do it."

Cal searched his mind for the right words to say. People's ability to lie to themselves was unlimited when it came to protecting the ones they loved. Olivia's brain hadn't allowed her to believe in her grandfather's guilt but it was now forcing her to confront the truth. He decided to say nothing. She might not be ready to hear the words he wanted to say. All he could do was be there to listen.

"I know what you're thinking," she said, letting her hands drop to her sides as her shoulders sagged. "I'm kidding myself, right? My grandfather cheated on my grandmother for years, and he treated Sadie horribly. He used her, he made promises he never intended on keeping and he pretended he was an honest, upstanding man in the com-

munity. He even attended church with us each Sunday."
She brought her fingers up to a delicate cross on a chain
she wore around her neck. "He gave me this necklace for
my twenty-first birthday, and I believed it was a symbol of
our shared faith and our commitment to following God's
teachings." She laughed sardonically. "You must think I'm
such an idiot for defending him all this time."

"You're not an idiot," he said. "You're a passionate de-
fender of your family, and that's commendable. Family
members are often complicated and messy, but we love
them anyway."

She took a deep breath, still pressing two fingers onto
the silver cross around her neck.

"The thing is," she started. "I always knew Nonno could
be lacking in kindness toward other people. I just pretended
I didn't see it because he was always so kind and loving
with me. He spoke badly about your parents all the time,
even though they didn't retaliate. He caused so many rifts
and divisions between staff at the café. We had a really high
turnover because he made such unreasonable demands."
She looked at Cal, as the fine rain collected on her brows
and lashes. "But the worst thing was that he came between
you and me. I've lately realized we could've been friends
all along without his dark influence casting a shadow over
us. He told me to dislike you, and I obeyed him."

She was correct in her assessment of Mario. He had
been the puppet pulling the strings behind the supposed
feud between their two families. The effect of his words
and actions had been toxic.

"When you're a child, you speak like a child, you understand like a child and you think like a child," he said,
referencing a piece of scripture. "No child is ever responsible for being taught bad behavior. This isn't your fault."

She looked so sad that his heart heaved for her. "But you're not a child anymore, and Mario isn't here. We can break those old patterns. It's not too late for us to be friends. We're making up for lost time, right?"

She summoned up a smile. "It's so hard to let go of the past. After Nonno died, I remember feeling such a sense of freedom, especially in the café. Suddenly, we could all laugh and joke behind the counter without him shouting at us to be quiet. I could employ people like Rosalie and build a team of happy staff. I was liberated without Nonno's constant presence in the background." She bowed her head. "I felt so disloyal for feeling that way, like I wasn't honoring his memory. So I tried extra hard to remember all the nice things about him. I told everyone what a good man he was, even when it was obvious he was a lot more complicated than that. I thought I was doing the right thing, but I was living a lie. He wasn't a good man and I'm tired of pretending he was. It's exhausting."

Her tears mingled with the falling rain and Cal wrapped his arms around her, feeling her hot breath on his neck where she rested her head on his collar. The scales had fallen from Olivia's eyes, but it seemed as though they'd been slowly falling piece by piece ever since Mario's death. She had been fighting the awful truth that life was better without her grandfather's malign influence. He hoped she now felt better after ridding herself of the pent-up stress and guilt she'd been carrying inside.

"You got this, Olivia," he said, stroking her wet hair. "Mario doesn't hold sway over your life anymore. You're strong, and you know your own mind."

"There's one thing he used to tell me all the time," she said, gripping his torso tight. "He'd say it at least once a week."

"What was it?"

"Never trust the word of a Mackenzie."

Cal let out a deep and mournful sigh. Mario had planted seeds of hostility in his granddaughter, then fed and watered them until they took root. Now Olivia was having to perform the difficult task of pulling up those roots.

"You can trust me," he said. "I promise. You know that, right?"

"I know it in my head, but I can't quite manage to feel it in my heart." She laughed lightly. "Or maybe it's the other way around. I'm trying to trust you, Cal. I really am, but it's hard."

"I understand." He continued to stroke her hair. "Take all the time you need."

"Can we go home now?" she asked. "I think a hot shower and an early night will make me feel a whole lot better."

"Sure."

She disentangled from his embrace, took a tissue out of her purse and began dabbing at the moisture on her face. Then she secured her wayward hair with an elastic from around her wrist. Her mascara had smudged beneath her eyes, and her hair had frizzed up in the cute way it always did in the rain. Olivia was at her most stunning when she wasn't trying.

"You look beautiful," he said, unable to stop the words spilling from his mouth.

"Shut up, Cal," she said with a weak smile. "I do not."

He watched her walk to his truck. Of course she didn't believe him. She'd been indoctrinated to never trust the word of a Mackenzie.

They had only just made it out of the bar's parking lot when the Pontiac's headlights loomed from behind in a sudden blaze. The car must've made a right turn from a junction as Cal passed, and it approached fast, emitting a loud roar from the engine.

"Oh no," he said, pressing the gas pedal. "The Firebird is back."

Olivia swiveled around in her seat, shielding her eyes from the glare of the headlights.

"Can we outrun it?"

"No, but we can outsmart it."

He turned sharply onto the highway that ran adjacent to the river. Plenty of sections of this road had become flooded over the last day or two. Some parts were shallow, but others were deep. Low vehicles didn't stand a chance of powering through the more serious floods, but his truck was built for such terrain.

A shot zinged overhead, and Olivia screamed. "He's shooting, Cal! He's shooting at us!"

"Stay calm," he said. "He can't drive and take aim at the same time. We're safe."

Cal drove at speed through the puddles on the road, activating his wipers to disperse the resulting torrent of water. Narrowing his eyes against the brightness of the headlights in the rearview mirror, he could just make out the silhouette of a man in the driver's seat of the Pontiac. One hand was on the wheel and the other was holding a handgun through the open window.

"I'm going off road," he said, worried about one of those stray bullets hitting a tire. "Hold on tight. It's gonna be a bumpy ride."

SEVEN

Olivia gripped the dash with both hands as the truck bounced over the bumps and potholes of the hillside. The wheels frequently slipped on the wet grass, forcing Cal to ease off the gas pedal to gain better traction. Their headlights could only illuminate a short distance ahead, so the occasional tree appeared ahead of them as if looming from nowhere, requiring Cal to yank the wheel hard to avoid the obstacle.

The Pontiac was doing a good job of staying on their tail, despite being unsuited for the uneven ground. But he seemed to be keeping both hands on the wheel now, which meant he could no longer take shots at them. He was clearly focusing all his attention on remaining close. Cal's truck hit a huge bump, sending Olivia jumping into the air. Her entire body left her seat, and her head struck the roof. She then landed with a thump and a scream.

"You okay?" Cal asked, training his eyes straight ahead.

"I'm okay," she said, rubbing the top of her head. "But I hear a rumbling sound. You hear it too, right?"

"Yeah," he said. "It's coming from the hillside."

The low rumble began to get louder. Olivia looked up to see the outline of several trees moving in the distance. The ground beneath them was shaking.

"Cal!" she shouted. "There's a landslide up ahead."

"I see it."

He maneuvered the car to face downward and made way for the road. The Pontiac was now alongside them, also trying to outrun the waterlogged earth heading their way. Olivia tried to get a good look at the driver, but the darkness, jerky movement and panic affected her ability to focus. She turned around to check the status of the slide, only to see a tree nudging their bumper. The truck went faster and faster, and the highway below was approaching at breakneck speed. Their downward trajectory was entirely controlled by the slide—Cal's attempts at steering seemed to have no effect at all.

The truck hit the concrete of the highway with a cushioned thump as the tires made contact with a harder and more stable surface. As the landslide continued its way across the road, Cal yanked the wheel back and forth repeatedly, finally gaining some traction on the mud. The branches of a tree scraped along the passenger side, and Olivia saw a huge, uprooted oak pass them by as if it were floating. She closed her eyes, praying for deliverance.

When she opened them again, Cal was driving on smooth clear highway once more and the landslide was behind them. She swiveled in her seat to locate the Firebird. The slide had deposited it on the opposite side of the huge mound of mud, and the vehicle sat there motionless, with the headlights blazing in the darkness.

"Let's get out of here," Cal said. "The guy has a gun, and we know he intends on using it."

Olivia watched him grip the wheel tight, as he flicked his eyes between the road ahead and the motionless car fading into the distance.

"That was close, huh?" she said with relief.

Cal let out a long, slow breath. "Way too close for comfort."

The community hall of Abbeywood Church was brimming with people but was surprisingly peaceful and hushed. Beds were lined up against each wall, and most children were already sleeping soundly while adults chatted quietly, folding laundry or checking messages on their cell phones. The landslide had blocked Olivia and Cal's main route home. The only detour path, over South Bridge, was also compromised due to a fallen tree. Hence, she and Cal were currently marooned in the church, which was providing temporary accommodations for flood victims. It looked like they'd have to stay the night. Olivia had updated her father with the news.

She walked into the hall to wait for Cal to finish making his own phone calls in the foyer. She immediately spotted Rosalie serving mugs of cocoa through a kitchen hatch in the wall. Rosalie waved enthusiastically, calling her friend over.

"What happened to you?" Rosalie asked. "You look like you jumped into a full bathtub with your clothes on."

While standing outside Clark's Wholesale Foods, Olivia had gotten soaked by the rain and was still dripping wet. She told her friend about the Pontiac and the landslide while removing her wet jacket and hanging it on the back of a chair. Then she teased off her sneakers at the heels and stood in her socks, wriggling her toes to bring sensation back. She was cold and shivery, and her feet were numb. Rosalie immediately came out from the kitchen and placed a blanket across Olivia's shoulders, before sitting her in a chair and handing her a wonderfully warming mug of cocoa.

"What a terrible thing to happen to you, Olivia," Rosalie said. "I'm so glad you're okay. Where's Cal now?"

"He's making some calls in the foyer. We can't go home until the fallen tree is removed from the riverside road. It looks like we'll have to bed down here for the night."

Rosalie crouched down next to Olivia's seat. "This is a great place to get stuck," she said with a smile. "We have snacks, a movie room, hot showers, clean clothes and terrible dad jokes courtesy of Pastor Brian." Rosalie called over to the pastor, who was stacking chairs in the corner. "Cal and Olivia are here. They're staying the night."

Brian ambled over with a smile on his face.

"Seeing the two of you here with blankets and cocoa makes me think of when you were teenagers, here for youth lock-ins. Do you know what I say when I put my car in Reverse?" he asked repeating one of his favorite jokes. He was obviously in high spirits.

The two women looked at each other and answered in unison. "Ah, this takes me back."

"I guess I told you that one already, huh?" the pastor said. "Don't worry. I have plenty more. I'll be with you in a few minutes to regale you."

After Brian returned to his duties, Olivia bent her head toward Rosalie's, not wanting to be overheard.

"I just cried on Cal's shoulder," she whispered. "And we hugged."

Rosalie, still kneeling by the chair, placed her palm on Olivia's knee. "Did it make you feel better?"

"Yeah," Olivia said, hearing the surprise in her own voice. "He was so kind to me. I feel bad for spending all those years being horrible to him. I just wish..." She stopped.

Rosalie knew her best friend's innermost thoughts. "You wish your grandfather hadn't taught you to hate the Mackenzies."

After Mario died, Olivia never told anybody about the complexity of the emotions stirred up by the loss, but she now wondered whether Rosalie had already spotted them.

"I've seen the way you've slowly changed and become more carefree since your grandfather died," Rosalie said, confirming Olivia's suspicions. "And I knew you'd soon figure out that Cal isn't your enemy. It's the total opposite in fact. You and Cal always had the best chemistry, and it was obvious you were fighting an attraction. When you kissed him at prom, I thought you two would finally start dating and fall in love. But you probably didn't want to incur the wrath of your grandfather."

"That's true," Olivia confirmed. "He would've hit the roof if he'd known I kissed Cal."

"But Mario's gone now, and you can make your own choices. You can choose Cal if you want."

Olivia wrinkled her brow. "Was it that obvious I always liked him in high school?"

Rosalie smiled. "Only to me. And the teachers. And the football team."

Olivia laughed and shook her head. "You never told me."

Rosalie shrugged. "Sometimes we have to wait until somebody's ready to hear the words we want to say."

"You sound just like Cal."

"Then he must be very sensible, not to mention charming and popular." Rosalie held an index finger in the air as if a thought had just occurred to her. "We can change his name from Conceited Cal to Clever Cal. How does that sound?"

Olivia laughed and drew Rosalie into a hug, endlessly grateful for her wonderful friendship and wise counsel. Her spirit had lifted. She felt a hand on her shoulder and looked up to see Pastor Brian standing over her.

"Cal just told me about your ordeal this evening," he said, his face full of sympathy. "And I want you to know that the church is here for you both whenever you need." He looked around the hall. "As you can see, we have an army of volunteers here, and they'd be glad to make sure you have whatever you need to get a peaceful night's sleep."

She stood up, seeing Cal chatting to some familiar faces across the other side of the hall.

"Is that Bobby Billingham?" she asked, pointing to a man making up a cot with fresh linens in the far corner.

"It certainly is," the pastor replied. "Bobby has been volunteering with us ever since the flood center opened. He takes a shift whenever he can."

Olivia watched Bobby work, wondering whether he was aware of his stepmother's unhappy marriage to his father, or of her reputation in town. Shaking herself free of the thoughts, she realized it didn't matter. If Bobby could put the past behind him, she could do the same thing.

"I'd like to help out," she said, as Cal came to join her. "Is there a job I can do?"

"Count me in too," Cal chimed in.

"There are a hundred and one things you could do," the pastor replied. "Follow me."

For the next two hours, Olivia washed and dried dishes, prepared breakfast rolls for the following morning and took part in nighttime prayers. When the hall was silent and dark, filled with sleeping people, she began to load the hall's washer with towels while Cal undertook a patrol of the exterior. News of the latest attack on Olivia and Cal spread fast. This had naturally caused worry among the hall's residents, so Cal had organized a few burly men to act as patrol guards to set people's minds at rest.

"You should go to bed, Olivia," Pastor Brian said, coming into the small laundry room. "It's late. Rosalie prepared a cot for you in the Sunday School room."

"I'll turn in soon," she said, closing the washer door and adding laundry powder to the drawer. "I just want to finish up here first. I've really enjoyed serving tonight. It's reminded me of what's important."

"I'm glad," the pastor said. "And I'm even more glad to see you and Cal getting along. I knew it would happen."

She smiled, standing up and stretching out her back. "We're building our bridges," she said. "But it's on ongoing process."

She began to unload the dryer and fold the clean sheets, while Brian assisted by taking the corners.

"I've been praying for that rift to heal for a long time. Now I just have one thing left to tick off my bucket list," he said with a twinkle in his eye. "I'd like to go swimming with sharks."

This came as a surprise to Olivia. "You would?"

"Yes, but it's a nonstarter because it costs an arm and a leg."

She groaned at the terrible pun, but her chest filled with love. Being here with her church family and with Cal felt like returning home after a long journey away. She was feeling lighter and more unburdened. Yet there were still two big issues left to resolve: the identity of mysterious man attacking her and the sale of Moretti's. She had not given up on the dream of owning her family's café. Her grandfather hadn't been perfect by any means, but he'd built the place from the ground up, and she'd loved the café for her entire life. Cal was still a week and a half away from signing on the dotted line, so she had time to make the place truly hers, the way she'd always wanted.

And that's exactly what she planned on doing.

Cal opened the door of the laundry room and inhaled the fresh smell of detergent. Olivia was sitting on the floor, cross-legged in front of the dryer, pairing socks. When she noticed him enter, she looked up, slightly startled.

"Sorry, I didn't mean to scare you," he said, dropping to the floor to sit next to her. "Pastor Brian told me I'd find you in here. He says you're determined to do the chores of fifty people before you go to bed."

"It's therapeutic," she said, continuing to match up the socks. "It takes my mind off everything that's happening."

"Bear's got his night patrol out looking for the Pontiac. It's a distinctive car so it should be easy to spot."

"Who's behind these attacks, Cal?" she asked. "When it all started, I thought the culprit must be the man who killed Sadie, but my mind has changed." She gripped a pair of sports socks tightly in her hand. "I've accepted that my grandfather probably did it, so there must be another reason this man is targeting me."

This was a big step for Olivia to take. An acknowledgment of Mario's guilt was a sign of how much she had grown in character recently.

"I don't have any idea who this guy is," he answered honestly. "I can only assume someone is spooked by the questions you've been asking."

"All this because I stirred up some gossip?" she said, sounding doubtful. "Would someone really kill for that?"

"We're still alive," Cal pointed out, but Olivia just shook her head.

"We've survived everything so far, but it could have easily gone another way. You know how close we came to not making it out of the car when we got trapped in the river."

It was a fair point. Some of the attacks, like the brick thrown through the window, had seemed mostly about scare tactics, but other attacks could easily have been fatal. Whoever this attacker was, they were open to murder.

"Maybe your grandfather had some help in hiding Sadie's body," he said. "And the accomplice is scared of being found out."

"That's possible. Do you think it could be Randy? Or Bobby? He was looking at me a little weirdly tonight."

"Try not to think about it," he said. "Otherwise, you'll end up seeing everyone as a suspect." He nudged her with his shoulder, hoping to cheer her up with humor. "Even Pastor Brian."

He was pleased to see her lips curl into a smile.

"If Pastor Brian wanted me dead, all he needs to do is lock me in a room and tell me jokes for hours on end. That's enough to destroy even the strongest of people."

"I hear you," he said, having been subjected to many of their pastor's one-liners. "I'm sure he buys them in bulk from the bargain bin at the comedy club in Granton."

She laughed and continued to match up the pile of jumbled socks. He decided to give her a hand and dug into the mess.

"Pastor Brian is pleased to see us getting along," she said, focusing on her task rather than on him. "I think he feels like some sort of matchmaker."

"He'd only be a matchmaker if we were dating, right?"

"Exactly. We're just friends."

He snuck a glance at her. Her color had risen. Perhaps she saw him as more than a friend. His own feelings had grown complicated too. Years ago, he never could have imagined sitting on the floor of the church laundry room with Olivia Moretti, pairing socks and chatting like old buddies. Life had a funny way of pulling these little surprises.

"Seeing as we're friends now," he started. "Does that mean you might reconsider my offer to stay in your job at Moretti's?" He raised a pair of balled-up socks. "Look how well we work as a team."

"I'm not sure that matching socks proves we can run a café together." She giggled. "Besides, the pair in your hands is mismatched. One is dark red while the other is burgundy."

He looked down at his hands. She was right.

"Okay, forget about the socks." He put them to one side to give her his full attention. "I promise to give you all the freedom you want in running Moretti's in Abbeywood. I'll be busy setting up new cafés anyway, so I wouldn't interfere with your day-to-day operations. You know the place inside out and your pastries are famous. We could negotiate a good salary."

She stopped what she was doing and fixed him with the deepest stare imaginable. The serious expression on her face proved that whatever she was about to say was important to her.

"I don't want to work for anybody, Cal. I want to be my own boss."

He nodded an understanding. He couldn't argue with her logic. He wanted to be his own boss too. Yet Olivia was unlikely to be successful in her application for a bank loan. Therefore, being the boss of Moretti's might not be possible for her.

"Okay," he said, unpairing his mismatched socks. "I get it."

"You're right about one thing, though," she said with a slight smirk. "I'm definitely a huge asset."

He threw back his head and laughed. Typical Olivia. Not only did she always get the last word, but she made it witty.

Olivia was cold and uncomfortable, sitting in a small beige room beneath an air-conditioning unit at Maple Valley Bank while the manager assessed her loan application. After having a short interview, she'd handed over her detailed business plan, alongside projected profit forecasts and expansion plans. Olivia figured that if Cal had grand plans to grow the Moretti brand across the state, then she could borrow his idea. The Moretti name had brand value— and as a member of the Moretti family, she was the most qualified to use it.

Cal was currently waiting for her in a coffee house across the street. They'd arrived at the Granton Coffee Emporium early, and Cal had bought her an iced tea to settle her nerves. Then he'd given her strong words of encouragement and enveloped her in a hug. She could still smell his cologne on her blouse. The scent was surprisingly comforting.

She'd been fortunate to be able to attend her appointment that morning, as a risky situation had developed in Granton. The Abbeywood River ran through the center of the town, but so far, Granton had escaped the floods that were afflicting its neighbor. However, a flood alert had now been issued for Granton, with a warning that the river might begin to spill over its defenses in a few days' time. When she and Cal had arrived in the town, they'd witnessed residents piling sandbags against doorways and purchasing copious amounts of bottled water from the stores. They were clearly preparing for the worst.

Olivia fidgeted in her seat, pulling the cuffs of her jacket over her wrists. She was wearing her most expensive items of clothing—an olive green pantsuit with an ivory silk blouse. As she squirmed, she found herself wishing she'd worn something looser and more comfortable. She'd chosen her sharply tailored outfit in order to impress the decision-makers, but she didn't think it was having the desired effect.

The door suddenly opened, and the young manager bustled inside, carrying a folder of papers.

"Thank you for your patience, Miss Moretti," he said, sitting behind his desk. "My colleague and I have taken a great deal of time and care going over your application this morning. We've both been impressed with the level of business acumen on display."

This was a good sign. "Thank you."

But the next word from his mouth caused Olivia's heart to sink.

"However," he said. "We've made the decision not to approve your loan today. It was a difficult choice to make because of your persuasive arguments, but we don't have access to the official business accounts. That means we can't see all your outgoings. Your supply of receipts and invoices is good, but it's not enough. And, of course, when we talked on the phone, we discussed the bank's concern about your lack of collateral."

"Yes, I know," she argued. "But I made a mitigating statement in my business plan regarding that. I would be prepared to pay higher interest *and* larger monthly payments." She pointed to the file he'd placed on the desk, on which her name was written in black marker. "It's all there in my business plan. The profits of the café are excellent, and it's been running for almost seventy years, so it's a solid investment with very little risk for the bank, even without collateral."

"I'm sorry, Miss Moretti." The manager was shaking his head. "I'd be happy to receive another application in a year's time. I recommend you begin saving ten percent of your monthly turnover and…"

He stopped midsentence because a wailing siren started up somewhere outside. They both jumped from their seats, and the manager rushed to the window to push aside the vertical blinds.

"It's the town's flood alarm," he said, ushering her toward the door. "The river must've breached. The mayor's office gave us a protocol to follow if this happens. Our security guard will lead you to the assembly point."

Olivia shook her arm free where he was holding it.

"I have somebody waiting for me across the street."

She tried to make way for the main door but was steered away by a tall guard, dressed in a brown uniform.

"Please exit via the side door," he said. "It's not safe to head out front."

Olivia was caught up in a throng of customers and clerks being shepherded toward a small exit door at the side of the building. As she moved, she felt her cell phone buzz in her purse. After struggling to unzip the bag and squeeze her hand through the opening, she pulled out the handset and pressed the answer button. It was Cal.

"Cal," she said in a panic. "They won't let me out the front door and I don't know where I'm being taken."

He sounded as panicked as she did.

"I've been told that part of the river wall just collapsed, and water is gushing through the town. The café floor is already under five inches of water." In the background, she could hear the yelps and cries of the customers. "I'm trying to get out but it's chaos here. The café owners have locked the doors and are trying to herd us upstairs. They think it's safer to wait for rescue on the second floor than to try to evacuate."

He broke off to argue with someone in his vicinity, telling them to open the door and let him leave.

"I'm going to an assembly point," Olivia said. "I don't know where it is, but I'll call you once I'm there." She now saw water seeping beneath the large, closed doors of the front entrance. "It can't be too far away, right?"

"I'll find you, Olivia. Don't worry. Stay somewhere public and you'll be fine."

She hung up the phone and slotted it back into her bag, before exiting the side door and finding herself in a narrow street, close to a bus station. That must be the assembly point. Cal could easily find her there. She fought her way to the security guard's side and tugged on his shirt.

"Is there where we wait to be collected?" she asked.

"No, this is where you board a bus to take you out of town." He pointed to a row of buses lined up in their bays. "They've been waiting here on standby in case of emergency. Where do you live?"

"Abbeywood."

"Get on Number Seven. That's the Abbeywood Route."

She tried to resist the flow of people propelling her forward. "I can't. I'm meeting a friend. He's taking me home."

"Everybody is meant to be evacuated in the event of a flash flood," he said, ignoring her protests. "Get on the bus, ma'am."

As she tried to swerve out of the crowd and turn back, she felt herself being guided firmly with a hand in the small of her back. Before she knew what was happening, she was sitting in a bus seat and being told to stay there. Yet she still protested.

"It's for your own good," the guard said. "You don't wanna die, do you? This is a serious situation."

She looked around in fear, as the seats around her filled with people, all of whom appeared relieved and grateful to be boarding a vehicle that would take them to safety. Olivia was the only person desperate to get off, because even if this bus was leading her away from the flood zone, it was still separating her from her protector—and potentially delivering her into the hands of her tormentor.

Cal was angry, frustrated and scared.

"You have to let everybody out," he said to the waitress of Granton's Coffee Emporium. "My name is Chief Caleb Mackenzie of the Abbeywood Fire Department. It's not safe to stay."

The young girl looked terrified, her wide eyes darting between Cal and her manager, who was an older woman holding a cell phone to her ear.

"My manager is asking the emergency services for advice," she said. "But she thinks it's a good idea to wait upstairs in the meantime." She pointed to the staircase all the other customers had ascended. All except Cal. "The water's rising."

"It's only knee deep right now," Cal said calmly. "But within ten minutes it'll be up to our waist or higher, making a rescue potentially hazardous. Let us leave now before it's too late."

A sudden and loud rap on the glass-fronted door caused Cal to jump. A Granton firefighter was standing outside with a radio in his hand.

"Open up," he yelled.

The manager hurriedly hung up the phone and used her key to unlock the door.

"Get everybody out," the uniformed firefighter ordered. "I see customers at the upstairs windows. You were meant to send people to the assembly point in the event of a river breach. What are you still doing here?"

"The water seemed to be rising too fast," the manager replied. "I didn't know what to do. I panicked."

"Let's go, people!" the fireman shouted over her head, alerting the people upstairs to his presence. "Get on the bus at the top of the street and it'll take you on a short trip to the bus station. From there, you'll be evacuated from the town center."

"My truck is in the parking lot on Vine Street," Cal said. "I need to go get it."

"Not possible," the firefighter said, pushing past him to reach the staircase, where people had begun to descend. "Vine Street is where the wall collapsed. You'll have to leave the vehicle there until we shore up the defenses. That'll take us a day at least."

Cal rushed out onto the sidewalk, wading through the water. The wail of the town's flood alarm still echoed through the air. He wondered if Olivia had reached the assembly point and whether he might be able to reach her before she was evacuated. He could see a series of small waves rippling down the street, lapping against the windows of stores and restaurants, as people raced to leave the scene. He had been trained in flood management, and it was obvious the water level was rising far more rapidly than anyone expected, being propelled by a large gap in the defenses. The pressure of the swollen river must've been too overwhelming for a weak spot in the concrete wall.

His cell began to ring in his pocket. The ringtone was "The Flight of the Bumblebee," which was the tune he'd assigned to Olivia. He yanked out the handset and answered the call.

"I'm on a moving bus," she said before he'd finished saying hello. "It's on Highway Four. We're stopping at various points to let people off."

"Where's the Abbeywood stop?"

"The Church Community Hall."

He breathed a sigh of relief. "Great. There are plenty of people there, and you'll be safe with them. I'm stuck in Granton right now, but I'll come meet you as soon as I can." He suddenly remembered why they had made the journey that morning. "How did the meeting go?"

Her silence spoke volumes. "I'm sorry, Olivia," he said. "I really am."

"It looks like you'll be the new owner of Moretti's after all," she said. "I'm sure you'll do a great job."

He waited for words of wisdom to strike him, so he could say something meaningful and supportive. But all he could think of was her pain and sadness at losing her precious café.

"I'll try my best," he said, hearing the inadequacy of the words. "To make you proud."

"I'm sure you will. I'll see you later."

After hanging up the phone, Cal joined the line of coffee house customers wading through the water, assisted by firefighters. They were heading for an idling bus at the end of the street. As he walked, he thought of several things he could've said to Olivia instead of uttering an inane platitude.

"You deserve the world on a plate," he whispered under his breath, causing the elderly woman in front to turn and stare at him oddly. "Joy will fill your life because you bring joy to others."

Why did he always think of such words when it was a moment too late?

Olivia jerked forward in her seat as the bus suddenly ground to a halt. The driver turned to the handful of people left in their seats and called out, "All Abbeywood riders get off here."

Olivia stood up. "But we're a mile from town."

"I've just learned that there's a landslide—I can't go any further," the driver replied. "I've been told to turn onto Route Eleven from here. You'll have to walk the rest of the way."

Olivia looked at the faces of the other passengers hopefully, but none of them seemed like they would be leaving the bus with her. Apparently, she was the only Abbeywood passenger.

"Could you at least go a little further on?" she asked the driver.

"My boss radioed me to say I'm not allowed to drive beyond this point," he replied. "There's no place to safely turn around once I reach the slide. My next stops are Franklin Junction and Holly Bridge. Are they any good for you?"

She didn't know anybody in either of those locations, and cell phone signal was patchy in this area, so she couldn't guarantee she could reach Cal or her dad to let them know where she was.

"No," she said. "I need to get back to Abbeywood."

The driver pulled the lever, and the door swung open. "Then you'll need to vacate the bus now. I'm sorry, ma'am, but I'm on a tight schedule. Once the bus is empty, I gotta get back to Granton immediately."

She sighed and walked down the steps to the side of the road. She held up her cell but wasn't surprised when she saw that she had no service. So she began walking, calculating the best route to avoid the slide. She'd likely have to walk over fields in her best suit and suede boots, but she'd make it work somehow. There wasn't any other option. Behind her, the bus turned at the crossroads and rumbled on its way toward Franklin Junction, leaving her entirely alone.

Typing out a message to Cal, she included a link to a tracking app on her phone and updated him on the situation. Once her cell connected with the intermittent signal, the message would reach him, and he could come get her in his truck. She suddenly stopped and placed a flat palm on her forehead as she realized that Cal likely wouldn't be able to retrieve his truck from the lot in Granton. He might even have gotten trapped in floodwaters. Cal was a fully trained firefighter, but that didn't guarantee that he'd be able to escape the danger with ease. With the water levels rising rapidly, he could have come to harm.

She shook away the thought and continued walking. Cal was fine. She was sure of it. Nonetheless, she sent up a silent prayer, asking God to protect him. The thought of losing Cal was awful. Somehow, he had recently established himself as someone important in her life. One day they were arguing like old rivals but the next they were sharing a joke like firm friends. And now she looked forward to seeing him. She might even love him.

She halted in her tracks. Did she just think that she *loved* Cal? That couldn't possibly be true. Sure, she thought he was cute and funny, but she thought the same thing about the mailman. There was more to love than that, right?

A little voice started up in her head—*he's also caring, honorable, safe and smart*.

"He's taking my café," she said, out loud, momentarily glad nobody was around to hear her talking to herself. "Can I trust him?"

Her inner voice was noncommittal—*wait and see*.

A car engine sounded behind her. This stretch of road was quiet, usually only being used by those heading to

Clark's Wholesale Foods. She turned and waved her arms, seeing Dennis heading her way in a store-branded truck. She waited for him to slow and activate the window, but he sped up, pretending not to see her. Then he sailed past, leaving her at the side of the road.

She sighed and watched his truck head into the distance, while a sinking feeling settled in her gut. Surrounded by nothing but forest and birds, she realized that in this location, nobody was around to hear her scream.

EIGHT

The day was muggy, with an overcast sky and a fine drizzle of rain. Angry black clouds in the distance warned of an approaching storm. Every now and again, Olivia saw a flash of lightning illuminate the dark clouds, bouncing inside them like a firefly trapped in a jar. Then the low, steady rumble of thunder would begin, causing her to pick up her pace on the asphalt. She didn't want to be trapped outside in a thunderstorm.

She stopped at a junction, wondering whether to turn right and head for the grocery store or continue to the community hall. The store was a little closer than the community hall, but the road to it was a dead end. She'd be stuck. And given the way Dennis had resolutely ignored her when she'd attempted to flag him down, it didn't seem likely he'd let her take shelter there and use the phone.

Making the decision to continue onward, she took off her jacket and folded it in the crook of her elbow, wishing she'd put a water bottle in her purse. She was getting hot. After walking a short distance, she heard another car engine echoing across the valley. Her blood ran cold. The noise was throaty and raw, clearly being emitted by a powerful car. An image of the Pontiac Firebird settled in her mind. She panicked and began running, searching for a safe place to hide. Yet she was trapped by a steep bank on one side and the river wall on the other. On the other side of the stone wall was the raging torrent of the Abbeywood River.

The engine sound grew louder and louder, until it was almost behind her. She glanced back and let out a yelp of fear. The Pontiac was tearing toward her at high speed. She raced toward a large tree on the shoulder of the road, dropping her jacket and purse before taking a running leap. She grabbed hold of a strong, low branch and used it like the uneven bars in gymnastics, swinging her body back and forth until she'd gathered enough momentum to hook her legs onto a higher branch. Then she sat on the thick tree limb, clinging onto the trunk, as the Pontiac tires squealed to a stop on the road directly beneath her. She gazed above, assessing whether she might be able to climb higher, not wanting to look down in case it triggered an episode of dizziness. In her peripheral vision, she saw a masked man exit the car. Then he made his way to the base of the trunk with something in his hand.

Bang!

He was shooting at her. The bullets zinged past, shredding leaves and twigs in their path. She almost lost her grip on the branch she was sitting on but managed to steady herself just in time. She now had no choice but to climb higher to conceal herself in the denser foliage. Her olive-green pants would hopefully act as camouflage, giving her a little extra protection. She found a higher, sturdy tree limb and sat on it with her back against the trunk. Then she bent her knees up to her chest, hiding as much of her ivory blouse as possible while holding a nearby branch. She was now as high as she dared go. A fall from this height would likely break bones or be fatal.

The shots rang out again, but it was clear the gunman

couldn't accurately pinpoint her. He shot at random, aiming a little higher than Olivia had climbed. She clamped her mouth shut to prevent a sound escaping. There was no way out of this situation. She was trapped within the dense leaves, curled up in a ball as her heart hammered in her chest. Her only hope lay with her attacker being scared away. As soon as Cal received her tracking data, he'd head over without delay, but she had no idea whether her cell had yet connected to a signal.

While the gunfire created a storm of noise around her, she prayed harder than she'd ever prayed before. As she had no ability to help herself in this situation, she placed herself in the hands of the Lord and asked for His mercy.

Bear slammed on his brakes as he turned a corner, and Cal saw a green jacket and leather purse lying in the middle of the road.

"Those are Olivia's things," Cal said. "But where is she?"

Both men jumped from the vehicle and began searching the area, calling out Olivia's name. Cal was glad to have his old friend there to help. Instead of boarding an evacuation bus out of Granton, he'd called the sheriff to come pick him up. It was on their return journey to Abbeywood that Cal's cell had pinged with Olivia's message about her thwarted attempt to reach the community hall. Her tracking app had then led him all the way to this exact location, but he could see no sign of her, except her jacket and purse.

"Shh," Bear said, bringing his index finger to his lips. "Listen."

Cal stopped in his tracks and turned up an ear. A woman was calling out from somewhere above his head. He scanned the treetops. Surely Olivia couldn't have scaled one of these large white ash trees that lined the side of the road?

He cupped his hands on either side of his mouth. "Olivia!"

Her reply was muffled but distinct. "I'm here, Cal. Directly above you, to the right."

He shifted his focus, and she came into view, sitting on a large tree branch with her legs dangling on either side. Her green pants and ivory blouse did a good job of concealing her in the dappled leaves.

"What are you doing up there?" he asked. "Are you hurt?"

"No. I'm fine. I just need to get the courage to climb down."

"What happened?"

"The Pontiac chased me on the road, so I had to hide," she said, pushing a leafy branch aside so he could see her more clearly. "The guy took potshots at me until a siren in the distance spooked him. He must've thought it was heading our way, and he left."

"One of my deputies responded to a traffic accident about thirty minutes ago," Bear said. "I heard the call come through the radio. That was probably the siren he heard."

"Can you get down?" Cal asked. "Or do you need me to come up there?"

"I'll be okay," she said, swinging her leg over the branch and tentatively placing her foot on the branch below. "I got up here, so I'm sure I can get down."

He watched her carefully find safe footholds on the tree limbs, and she slowly descended. When she was on the lowest branch, he stretched out both arms, indicating his readiness to catch her. Without hesitation, she jumped and landed right where she was meant to—in his arms. Then he placed her on her feet and held her tight, feeling her heart pounding beneath her blouse. The descent from her high position was likely more terrifying than she was willing to admit.

"You're okay," he said, stroking her hair. "You're safe."

"The gunman knew exactly where to find me," she said breathlessly. "Dennis passed me in his truck a few minutes before the Pontiac showed up. He could've made a call to my stalker to give him my location."

"Or the stalker could've hacked the tracking app on your cell phone."

She gasped. "I hadn't thought of that."

"I'll check it for malware, just to be on the safe side."

He withdrew from the embrace to pick up her purse and jacket from the ground.

"Let me take a look at it, Cal," Bear said. "I've done a malware training course, so I know what to look for."

"Thank you, Bear," Olivia said, taking her purse from Cal to pull out her cell phone. "I'll unlock it for you."

After handing the phone to Bear, the sheriff returned to his cruiser to sit inside and concentrate on the task. Meanwhile, Olivia walked to the riverside wall and leaned against it, letting her purse and jacket fall to the ground once more. Her body language was defeated.

"It was smart thinking to send me a link to track you," Cal said, trying to buoy her with a compliment.

"I'm smart enough to outwit a crazed attacker, but not smart enough to be approved for a loan to buy Moretti's." Her shoulders dropped in sadness. "I'm all outta options now. In ten days' time, you'll be signing the paperwork and running the show."

"I'm sorry, Olivia," he said, wishing she'd gotten the green light. "I know what this means to you."

She forced a smile that he suspected was for his benefit. "It won't be easy seeing Moretti's in someone else's hands, but at least it's someone like you. The customers will love you. I just know it."

"Will *you* love me?"

The words tumbled out before his brain had a chance to catch up with his mouth. He hadn't meant to say it, but now he'd asked the question, he really wanted to know the answer. He'd been fighting strong feelings for Olivia for a while, and he wondered if there was any chance she was going through the same thing. But her prolonged silence was torturous, and he couldn't stand the discomfort any longer. Maybe he could save himself from embarrassment by making the comment into a joke.

"I mean, if the customers love me, then you're bound to feel the same way, right?" He laughed. "I'm a very love-able guy."

She stood up straight and shifted on her feet awkwardly. "You really are, Cal. I never thought I'd say those words but they're true."

They stood in silence while the thunder rumbled across the sky, both seemingly lost in their own thoughts. Finally, the moment was broken by Bear, who was calling from his cruiser.

"I didn't spot anything malicious on the cell phone," he said. "Let's go take a statement and investigate what happened here. We've got a bad guy to find."

"We sure do," Cal said, putting his arm around Olivia. "And we should let Leonardo know you're okay."

Olivia leaned her head on his shoulder, and he resisted the urge to plant a kiss there. She was hurting, and he desperately wanted to make it better. But the only thing she wanted in life was to be the boss of Moretti's and he simply couldn't make that happen.

Or could he?

He'd been thinking of it as an either/or—either he'd take over or Olivia would. But maybe there was a way they could be partners instead? He and Olivia made a good team lately, and there was something special happening between them. If he invited her into the negotiating room, would she consider working with him in return for a stake in the business?

There was only one way to find out.

The thunderstorm drew ever closer, darkening the sky and whipping the wind into eddies. Cal was at the Redwood Reservoir, undertaking some vital assessments of the cracks in the dam before the heavy rains came. The splits in the earth hadn't gotten any worse and the dam wasn't in imminent danger of failure, but he'd need to come out and reevaluate the following day. He'd arranged to meet with an operative from the New Hampshire Dam Bureau at the same time. The organization had been struggling to cope with unprecedented demands created by the recent flooding, but Cal had been assured of their commitment to assessing the danger tomorrow.

Just as he was packing away his camera and tripod, he saw two dark figures heading his way. Both were hunched against the light rain, with hoods pulled over their heads. After everything that had happened with Olivia, he was immediately on his guard. He had borrowed a truck from the fire station and headed straight to the reservoir on his own, not considering he might be in danger in such a remote location.

He picked up a large rock from the ground and held it at his side, waiting for the men to show themselves more clearly. When they lifted their heads, he saw the faces of Randy Billingham and Dennis Clark. He eyed them warily. There was no reason for them to be at the reservoir. In fact, it was a restricted area.

"What are you two doing here?" he called, keeping hold

of the stone by his side, just in case of trouble. "There's a storm coming. You should be at home."

"We heard the dam has cracks in it," Dennis said, continuing to approach. "And we're worried about our homes being flooded if it breaks. We wanted to look for ourselves."

Cal held up a hand. "Stop! That's close enough."

Randy and Dennis exchanged a glance.

"What do you think we're gonna do, Cal?" Dennis asked. "Attack you?"

"I'm just making sure of my safety," Cal replied. "You seem to have a harsher idea of how neighbors should treat each other than I do. You passed Olivia on the road earlier today and you failed to stop for her. She was chased by a man shortly afterward. He took shots at her while she tried to hide. She's unhurt, but it's no thanks to you."

"I passed Olivia in my truck?" Dennis asked in apparent surprise. "Are you sure? I haven't seen anybody out walking."

Cal narrowed his eyes. "Who said anything about her walking? And I don't recall mentioning you being in your truck either."

Dennis pinched his lips. "I'm always in my truck when I'm on the road, and I assumed she'd be on foot if she was looking for help." He clicked his tongue. "I didn't see anybody. I must've been focused on getting back to my store with supplies. It's a busy time."

Cal didn't believe a word Dennis said.

"Do either of you know someone who owns a vintage Pontiac Firebird?" he asked. "It's black with two white stripes on the hood."

Randy's eyes widened in what looked like shock or surprise, and he stumbled slightly. He clearly knew this vehicle.

Dennis was the first to shake his head. "It doesn't ring any bells with me."

Randy quickly followed suit. "Me neither."

"We should go," Dennis said, jerking his head down the hillside. "The fire chief doesn't want us here."

Cal dropped the stone in his hand, certain now that Dennis and Randy wanted to evade him rather than attack him.

"Bear has already traced the Firebird to a dealership who sold it years ago," he said loudly, ensuring he got their full attention. He was bluffing, of course. Bear had no information on the car at all. But they'd have no way of knowing that. "The dealer will be supplying him with the details of the purchaser later today, so if either of you is lying, Bear will want to know why. And you know what Bear is like. He's a gentle giant but he's pretty scary when he finds out somebody's been telling lies."

Randy shoved his hands deep into his pockets, like a toddler caught with his hand in the cookie jar.

"All right," he said petulantly. "I bought a car like that for Sadie the day before she vanished. It was a gift to show her how much she meant to me. It cost me a fortune, but she was pleased as punch with it."

"What happened to it?" asked Cal.

"How should I know?" Randy responded. "It disappeared along with Sadie. I assumed she took it to New York."

"Well, she clearly didn't, did she?" Cal said. "How could she take it to New York when she was buried in the cellar of Moretti's Café? Who took her car after she was killed?"

"Why are you asking me?" Randy yelled, suddenly angry. "Mario Moretti killed her. He's the only person who might know the answer."

Cal turned his attention to Dennis. "Do you know who has the car now?"

Dennis held up his hands. "Hey, man, I don't know anything about a car like that. I've never even seen it before."

"What about Bobby?" Cal asked Randy. "He was twenty-one when Sadie disappeared, so he'd remember the car, right? He might know where it went after she vanished. Maybe he sold it. Or maybe he kept it in a garage somewhere."

"I'm telling you, the car disappeared the same time as Sadie," Randy said, making a jabbing motion in the air with his index finger. "You leave my son out of this. He's been through enough already."

"We'll get to the bottom of it eventually," Cal said, hoping they'd take it as a warning about withholding information. "The truth always wins in the end."

The rain was falling heavily, and peals of thunder rumbled around the town like giant marbles. Olivia sat in the sheriff's office next to Cal, acutely aware of his arm pressed against hers. Since he'd asked her whether she loved him, a shyness had settled between them. His question had taken her off guard, and she'd been stunned into silence. Even though he'd tried to pass off the comment as a joke, she could see the emotion in his eyes.

She hadn't answered him because she simply didn't know what to say. The feelings she'd developed for Cal were unfamiliar to her. She wanted to be with him all the time. She loved the sensation of being in his arms. She could recall every inch of his face at any given moment. This certainly felt a lot like love, but she didn't have any experience in that department, so how would she know? And was she really in the right frame of mind to deal with more turmoil? She'd been attacked, repeatedly, and her life was still in danger. And on top of that, the loss of Moretti's still made her heartsick, even if she had learned to accept her path with humility.

She comforted herself with the reminder that her faith in God was a rock on which she rested, and that Cal shared her strong beliefs. His plan to expand the Moretti's brand was good, and his idea to funnel the profits into a homeless shelter was honorable. He deserved her full support even if the loss of her wonderful café made her weep. She suspected many tears would be shed over the coming months, or even years.

Bear took a seat behind the desk in front of them, placing a pile of scribbled notes on the surface. Since Cal had informed him that Randy admitted to purchasing the Firebird for Sadie, the sheriff had been making a lot of calls.

"A contact at the DMV located the last known license plate of Sadie's Pontiac Firebird," he said. "The plate expired twenty-nine years ago, so whoever took the car isn't keeping the paperwork updated." He scratched his head. "I've never seen this car on local roads. It's weird that it suddenly pops up now, out of the blue."

"Maybe it's been in a garage somewhere?" Olivia suggested. "Somebody might've kept it as a memory of Sadie."

"Randy," Cal said firmly. "For all his faults, he really loved Sadie. He said she was overjoyed to get the car, so I think he's the most likely person to have it as a keepsake."

Bear shook his head. "Randy is adamant he doesn't have the car. Bobby too. They say they haven't seen it in thirty years. When I spoke with Randy this morning, he said Mario probably took it and hid it somewhere, considering Mario was the one who likely killed her. People might have suspected something was up if her car didn't disappear at the same time she did."

A few days ago, a comment like that regarding the guilt

of her grandfather would've set Olivia rushing to defend him, but she had since grown into a new person. With Cal's help, she had come to terms with the truth and stepped out of her grandfather's shadow. She dropped her hand to Cal's side between their chairs and silently slipped it into his. He squeezed her fingers tight.

"My grandfather might've taken the car," she said, thankful for Cal's warm touch. "But I never saw it at the house or at the café. I guess he could have sold it or given it away, but that doesn't explain why it's been hidden away all this time."

"Does this mean you've accepted that Mario is probably responsible for Sadie's murder?" Bear asked, his tone gentle.

"Yes," she said. "I've realized a lot of things lately, and my grandfather's guilt is one of them. I won't be asking any more questions or bothering any more folks in Abbeywood." She sighed. "I don't think the attacks will stop, though. Whoever's targeting me is obviously hiding a secret so bad they can't risk letting me live."

Bear and Cal exchanged a solemn look, as they both acknowledged what was at stake. Olivia's life was on the line.

"I'm sorry if I've been hard on you about this case, Olivia," Bear said. "I only wanted to keep you out of danger."

"I understand," she said. "I was hard on you too. I should've known better."

The sheriff leaned on his desk with his forearms, hanging his head.

"I feel obliged to come fully clean at this point," he said quietly. "Thirty-two years ago, I pulled over Sadie's Volkswagen, and she tested positive for DUI. She was crying and begging me not to arrest her. She said it would ruin her life." He looked up with eyes full of remorse. "I knew her backstory and I felt sorry for her, so I let her off with a warning. I shouldn't have done it and I've been ashamed of myself ever since. That's why I've been so reluctant to talk about my relationship with Sadie. We began an affair shortly after her DUI, and I didn't want anybody to find out about either of those things. I was afraid the truth would come out."

Olivia took a moment or two to digest the words and appreciate how difficult it must've been for the sheriff to say them.

"Thank you for being honest," she said. "I think it's safe to say we've all made mistakes over the years, but the important thing is that we learn from them, right?"

"It sure is," the sheriff replied as the phone on his desk began to ring. "Excuse me, guys."

Olivia turned to Cal as the sheriff picked up the call.

"I should be getting home," she said. "Nonna's dementia has gotten much worse in the last few days, and Dad needs my support."

"Sure." He grabbed his keys from the desk. "Let's go."

Bear rose from his seat and also picked up his keys.

"The flooding is creeping further up Main Street," he said. "Nobody is in danger, but your firefighters need help laying sandbags against the doorways of local businesses. I'll allocate every spare deputy and pitch in myself."

"I'll come on down after dropping off Olivia," Cal said, as they both followed Bear to the exit. "Thanks for helping out, Sheriff."

Bear opened the door and hurried to his car, holding his jacket over his head. Olivia stepped outside and zipped up her raincoat while standing beneath the small roof jutting out over the doorway. The rain was hammering in sheets, and she pulled her hood over her head in readiness. Then she noticed Cal watching her with a smile on his face.

"What?" she said. "You're looking at me weirdly."

"I have a proposition for you, and I think now is the time to make it."

She was intrigued. "What is it?"

"I'd like you to be my business partner at Moretti's—fifty percent each." He held up his hands, fingers splayed. "I'd put up all the money, while your investment would consist of café expertise, family name continuity and baking skills." He smiled. "We can both be the boss."

Olivia felt her mouth drop open in shock at this huge and unexpected bombshell.

"You don't have to do this, Cal," she said when she found her voice. "You don't have to feel sorry for me."

"This isn't a pity offer. This is a business decision, based on what's best for Moretti's. You know the brand better than anybody, and you're the best pastry chef I'll ever find. I'd be a fool not to want you by my side."

Cal's proposal should've been music to her ears. It was her dream to remain at Moretti's as the manager and owner. But Cal's investment would far outweigh hers. He would be stumping up all the cash, while her pockets contained nothing but mothballs. It didn't feel right.

"This is the kindest thing anyone has ever done for me," she said, pressing two flat palms onto his chest. "But I can't let you do this."

"I'm not doing it just for you," he said. "I'm doing it for me too. Please take some time to think about it. I feel like we could achieve great things together. With my levelheadedness and your tenacity, we could conquer the world." He laughed. "But we'll start with New Hampshire." He cupped her cheek and butterflies erupted in her belly. "You're smart, capable and caring, and I can't imagine not being able to see you every day."

His beautiful words took her breath away. All she could do was stare at him, blinking fast, listening to the sound of the rain hitting the small shelter over their heads. Before she knew what she was doing, she kissed him.

And he kissed her back.

Cal walked into the living room of the Moretti family home to find Leonardo trying to calm Francesca. Cal didn't understand a word of what the elderly lady was saying, but he knew the language was Italian and it was clear that Francesca was deeply agitated. Leonardo appeared to be struggling to respond to her in her native tongue, though he frequently reverted back to English as he spoke soothing words.

"My Italian is too rusty," Leonardo said to Cal, as Olivia hugged her grandmother while singing an Italian song softly into her ear. "My mother is starting to forget her English vocabulary these days. The doctor said it might happen as the dementia progresses. I wish I'd taken more care to retain my Italian fluency."

"She's talking about Nonno," Olivia said, settling her grandmother into a chair and tucking a blanket around her legs. "She's saying something about him losing everything." She looked at her father. "Your Italian is better than mine, Dad. Is she talking about the sale of the café? Does she understand what's going on?"

Francesca picked up the blanket and threw it to the carpet, continuing to mutter in Italian, while gesticulating with her hands. Cal had never seen the old lady look so disheveled. Her white hair was wild and her clothing in disarray.

"I'll take her upstairs," Leonardo said, helping his mother out of her chair. "She's always calmer in her bedroom."

Cal moved forward to assist Leonardo while Olivia watched with concern.

"Dad," she said. "What does *omicido* mean. She's saying it a lot."

"I don't know, Olivia," her dad replied, as Cal helped in walking Francesca to the door. "Like I said, my Italian is rusty." He patted Cal's arm. "I've got it from here, Cal. Thank you for taking care of Olivia these past few days. You've been a Godsend."

"Dad!" Olivia called after her father as he walked his mother up the stairs. "*Omicido* sounds like the word homicide. Is that what it means?"

"Leave it alone, Olivia," Leonardo called back. "Stay with Cal and let your grandmother rest."

Cal returned to the living room, and Olivia dropped into an armchair by the fire, looking shaken.

"All this time, I thought Nonna didn't know what was going on," she said, covering her eyes. "But she was listening to all the conversations about Sadie's murder. She understands more than I realize. I should've been more careful."

Cal knelt to the carpet beside her and took her hands from her eyes, laying them on her knees before pressing them reassuringly with his own.

"You have no idea what's on your grandmother's mind," he said. "Her brain isn't functioning like it used to. When she's rested awhile, she'll probably have forgotten about what was bothering her."

"I wish she could talk to me like she did before dementia set in. I wish she could tell me what she's thinking. What if she's angry with us for selling the café? I couldn't bear to feel like we've disappointed her."

"You've done nothing wrong, Olivia," Cal said. "The decision to sell the café wasn't yours in the first place."

He waited for her to mention his business proposal. Or perhaps their kiss. But she stared at her hands silently, twining her fingers. During the car ride from the sheriff's office, she'd been quiet, as if mulling things over in her mind. He'd allowed her the time and space to fully consider whether she wanted to accept his offer.

"Tell me what you're thinking," he said, unable to remain silent any longer.

"Did you mean what you said?" she asked. "About wanting to see me every day."

"Of course I did. I love being with you." The words *I love you* teetered on the tip of his tongue, but he didn't have the confidence to set them free. "And our kiss meant a lot to me."

"Me too," she said. "I care so much about you, Cal. That's why I won't allow you to bankroll me as a partner in Moretti's. You've worked too hard to throw away fifty percent of your stake on me."

In his mind, he wasn't throwing anything away. By bringing Olivia on board, he would be gaining an advantage, not just in a practical sense but in an emotional sense too. She made each day brighter.

"You're worth the investment," he said, watching her eyes become moist. "I believe in you. I really do."

She stood up, and his hands slid from her knees. "I'm keeping you from your job," she said, changing the subject. "Your crew is laying sandbags and you're here with me, talking business."

He stood up. "Your grandfather told you to never trust a Mackenzie. Is that what's holding you back?"

"No," she said. "I trust you. Implicitly."

"Then be my partner?"

She shook her head. "I have nothing to offer you."

"You're all I need."

"You're sweet," she said, backing away from him. "But you're not thinking straight, and you'll regret giving away so much. I'm saving you from yourself, Cal."

With that, she left the room.

The explosion was booming, shaking the house with such force that Olivia felt her bed move. She threw back the covers and raced onto the landing, almost colliding with her father at the top of the stairs.

"What was that?" she asked. "Was it an earthquake?"

"I don't think so," her father said, securing his robe with a cord around his waist. "There's a fire on the driveway. It looks like something exploded."

He pointed to the front door, where orange and yellow flames could be seen flickering through the frosted glass panel. Olivia and her father shared a worried glance before both rushing down the stairs and heading into the living room to look through the window. There in the driveway was Sadie's Pontiac Firebird, fully alight, sending flames rising into the dark sky. Although heavy rain continued to fall, it seemed to have no effect on the fire, and Olivia could feel the strong heat passing through the windowpane. She pulled her father back from the glass as he called 911 and explained the situation.

"The fire department is on its way," he said, returning to the window to peer out. "Why would somebody do this?"

"Because they have a terrible secret," she said. "And I've obviously gotten too close."

"Oh, Olivia," her father said, rubbing her eyes. "Maybe it's a good idea if we put the house on the market and…"

He stopped and his eyes widened in horror. Olivia turned to see her grandmother reaching for the lock on the front door. She was wearing her nightgown and slippers and

must have been awoken by the noise. Usually frail and un-
steady on her feet, she was now walking with purpose, as
if the sound of the explosion had filled her with adrenaline.

"No, Mom, no!" Leonardo yelled as he lurched forward
with an outstretched arm. "Don't open the door."

But she'd turned the lock and pulled down the handle
before either of them could reach her. Leonardo managed
to catch hold of his mother's wrist after she'd taken a couple of steps on the driveway.

"Fuoco," she said, using the Italian word for fire, while
shielding her eyes from the glare.

"Come back inside," Leonardo said, steering Francesca
toward the front door while Olivia stood in the doorway,
feeling the intense heat of the flames.

A sense of unease settled over her as she watched her
father gently lead her grandmother by the arm. When a
masked man appeared from the side of the house and rushed
toward them, she almost felt like she should have known it
would happen. But she was terrified, nonetheless. Both she
and Leonardo let out a scream as the man pushed Olivia
inside the house, using two flat palms on her chest. She
staggered backward and fell onto the bottom step of the
stairs, watching him enter and lock the door behind him.

Then she saw the glint of a metal blade in his hand, and
her blood ran cold. She picked herself up from the floor
and ran for her life.

NINE

Olivia ran into her bedroom and slammed the door shut, bolting it. As heavy kicking resounded on the door, she entered the adjacent bathroom and turned the thumb lock. This locking mechanism might hold for a minute or two, but it wouldn't be enough to save her. Her father's gun was in a locked drawer, and she didn't have time to reach it, so her best chance of survival was to escape. Her dad was almost certainly trying to gain access to the house right now, but without a key he didn't stand a chance. The place was like Fort Knox thanks to the security upgrades the church had paid for. Even the new windowpane was reinforced glass.

She heard her bedroom door fly open with a crack. Very quickly, blows began raining on the bathroom door, as hard, heavy kicks thudded through the small space. Thankfully, this bathroom was a shared space between Olivia and her grandmother, so there was another door on the opposite side, which led into Francesca's bedroom. Olivia darted through it and slipped into the hallway. As she descended the stairs with quick and light feet, she heard the bathroom door finally give way. She only had seconds before the masked attacker realized she had evaded him.

She reached the front door and fumbled with the lock.

Her hands were shaking, and she heard the man reach the top of the stairs behind her.

"No, no," she muttered to herself as she pressed the handle, only to find the door wouldn't open. In her haste, she must've rotated the thumb lock twice, unlocking and re-locking it again.

Fumbling to turn it once more, she felt a hand grab hold of the collar of her pajama top and yank her backward. She flew through the air and landed on the wooden floor of the hallway. She slid along the shined boards before colliding with the skirting. Her shoulder jarred against the hard surface, and she cried out in pain. But she had no time to focus on anything but surviving. She jumped up immediately, pivoting on the balls of her feet to enter the kitchen. Seeing the knives lined up in the block, she selected the biggest one and ran behind the large dining table. There she held the steel blade in front of her.

"Don't come any closer," she said, willing her hands to remain still. "I don't want to hurt you, but I'll do whatever it takes to protect myself."

Despite being unable to see his face behind the ski mask, she knew the man was smiling. He stood in the doorway of the kitchen, straightening to his full height as if to emphasize that her size and strength were no match for his own. And he was right. If he got close enough for her to strike, it was very likely he'd be able to overpower her before she could do any damage. She glanced around for a route of escape. Just to her right was the kitchen door, which led into the backyard, but it was locked, and all the keys were kept on a hook in the hallway, far out of reach. She offered up a prayer as the man advanced upon her, holding his knife purposefully in his hand. She would stand her ground and fight to her last breath.

Then she heard a key turn in the lock of the back door. Through the frosted glass, she saw a figure on the other side, and relief flooded her body when Cal appeared in the doorway. She'd forgotten he had a key. After the brick had been hurled through the window, her father had given him a key as a security precaution. That key fit both the front and back door, and Cal had wisely chosen the back door to make his entrance. His nostrils flared when he saw the masked intruder.

"Go stay with your father," he said to Olivia, walking into the middle of the kitchen as the intruder retreated slowly, clearly uncertain of what to do. "And wait for the police. Your dad called 911."

The masked man began swiping his blade through the air wildly, and Cal ducked and weaved out of the way. Olivia was concerned about his safety, as he appeared to be unarmed, so she dithered in the doorway, still clutching the large knife.

"Go, Olivia!" Cal yelled. "I got this."

She turned and stepped onto the tiled patio in the yard, instantly colliding with her father, who seemed to have aged ten years since she last saw him. Her grandmother was not by his side.

"Oh, Olivia!" he exclaimed, hugging her. "I was terrified for you. Cal rushed here after I called his cell, and he told me to wait outside until the police arrive. He's not on night duty, so he's not part of the fire station's response team. He gave me his gun in case of trouble." He glanced at the weapon in his hand. "I'll go help him." He pointed to the back of the yard, where Francesca was sitting in a swing chair beneath a tree. "You sit with your grandmother and reassure her."

Olivia dropped the knife to the ground and grabbed her

father's hand. "No, Dad, don't interfere. Cal wants us to stay out of the way."

Leonardo withdrew his hand from hers. "It's not right, Olivia. I must step up."

"Please, Dad," she pleaded, hearing a scuffle ensue inside. Crockery and pots were falling to the floor as Cal yelled for the culprit to stop resisting. "You might get hurt."

"I can't do nothing. This is my house, and I should defend it."

Her father marched through the door in his slippers and robe, yelling out warnings about his right to protect his home. Cal shouted something unintelligible in response, and Olivia tried to encourage her father to come back outside. She switched her gaze between the commotion in kitchen and her grandmother on the swing chair. Francesca, alerted by the disturbance, pushed herself to stand and Olivia called out across the lawn.

"Stay there, Nonna! Don't come to the house."

The voices in the kitchen merged with one another, as a chaos unfolded. Leonardo, raising the gun too close to the intruder, was shoved to the floor, and the gun skittered across the linoleum. Cal was thrown off balance by the tumble. The masked man swung wildly with his blade as Cal staggered among the broken crockery. The intruder then used the distraction to sprint for the open kitchen door. Olivia jumped out of the way as he fled, and she raced across the dewy grass to stand with her grandmother. Together, they watched the man vault the gate at the side of the house and disappear.

Above the roof, the smoke from the burning Pontiac rose into the sky, and a heavy smell of gasoline hung in the air. Olivia put her arm around Francesca, as the sound of sirens grew ever closer. When Cal appeared in the doorway, he looked over at her and mouthed "You okay?"

She gave him a thumbs-up, but she wasn't okay. She didn't know if she'd ever be okay again.

Would this threat ever end?

Cal handed a cup of coffee to Olivia, and she cradled it in her hands, blowing on the surface. She was sitting on a lawn chair in the backyard, trying to find some peace in among the bustling activity around her. Cal's night crew had extinguished the flames and were now examining the improvised explosive device that had been used to cause the blast. The shell of the vehicle smoldered on the driveway, while the residents of neighboring properties gathered round to stare at the scene. Despite the time being only 6:00 a.m., everyone was wide awake and chattering about the attack on the Morettis' home during the night.

"You need to keep warm," Cal said, spreading a blanket across her shoulders before sitting next to her. "It's chilly."

She looked skyward. "At least it's stopped raining."

"For a little while," he said ominously.

He sighed. Today's forecast was the worst yet and could cause major problems at the reservoir dam. He'd already met with a representative from the Dam Bureau, and the situation was now being monitored several times a day by a team of experts. An evacuation order of Redwood Estates might be unavoidable, but the decision was thankfully now in the hands of state officials. It was one duty he could scratch off his list.

"Who is this maniac attacking me, Cal?" Olivia asked. "And what's he·so scared of me finding out?"

"Sadie had a very complex past," Cal replied. "Maybe she was involved in something illegal like fraud or drugs, and this man is trying to protect himself from incrimination. Whatever he wants to cover up, it's got to be serious."

"Do you think my grandfather was involved too? I feel like I never fully knew him."

"I don't know. I never really knew him at all."

"I don't know if anyone did," she said. "He didn't have many friends. Customers didn't come to Moretti's for his wit and charm. They came for the pastries."

"They *still* come for the pastries," he said. "You're the best pastry chef in the county, maybe even the whole state."

"Nonno taught me well." She took a sip of coffee. "That's one thing I can thank him for."

Olivia leaned against Cal and rested her head on his shoulder. The steam from her coffee rose up into the air, filling it with a pleasant smell that Cal associated with his family's café. He'd worked at Mackenzie's straight out of high school, learning the ropes and becoming adept at cooking all kinds of savory dishes. Meanwhile, Olivia was learning the ropes from Mario at Moretti's, trying to outdo the Mackenzies by frequently introducing new and exciting desserts. Olivia always had the edge when it came to mouth-watering menus, and Cal admired her for her creativity.

"Mackenzie's could never compete with Moretti's on pastries," he said. "I can't make a croissant to save my life."

She laughed. "Croissants are French. Italians call them cornettoes. The key is fresh yeast, the freshest you can get."

"Do you see what I mean about your expertise?" he said. "How will I find anybody as talented as you?"

"You'll figure it out."

She was still clearly set against the possibility of a partnership, and he didn't press her on the matter. He wanted to respect her boundaries.

"Do you remember the time you brought cupcakes into school to celebrate Rosalie's sixteenth birthday?" he asked.

"Of course." Her tone was firm but playful. "How could

I forget? Somebody stole a cupcake from the box and put it on Mr. Shankland's chair in math. He got frosting all over the seat of his pants." She lifted her head to look at him sideways while he suppressed a smile. "And I got bawled out for it because I was the one holding the box."

"It was me," he said, holding up his hands. "I took one while you were distracted."

"I managed to figure that out for myself. I was assigned detention after school, but Mr. Shankland decided to let me off the hook with just a warning."

"I went to see him at recess, and I owned up to the prank," Cal said. "I got the detention instead."

"Really? You owned up to it?"

"Sure I did. I know I teased you a lot and joked around, but I never wanted you to be hurt by any of it. I just wanted you to notice me."

"Well, it worked," she said. "I noticed you all right."

He turned his head so their eyes could meet. "You never noticed me in the way I wanted you to notice me. Not until prom night."

She leaned forward to place her coffee cup on the table. Then she took his hand and sandwiched it between her own.

"I always hated it when you teased me about our kiss, because you were annoyingly right about everything. I enjoyed it. A lot. Nobody else could ever match up. I pretended it was no big deal, because we were meant to hate each other, right?"

"I never hated you," he said, bringing his lips close to hers. "It was the opposite, in fact."

He pressed his mouth onto hers and she responded to his kiss, tilting her head and closing her eyes. He found himself lost in the moment, forgetting where they were.

When she finally pulled away, she was smiling, looking more beautiful than ever.

"What does this mean?" he asked, needing to know where he stood. "For us?"

"I don't know," she replied. "I'm trying not to overthink it because the situation is complicated."

He understood what she was referring to. He was buying her beloved family café and while he still hoped they'd be able to work out a partnership, that wasn't a certainty. She might find the situation too painful.

"Let's just focus on the here and now," he said, brushing a curl from her face. "Rather than worrying about the future."

"Sounds good to me."

Their lips met again, and everything else melted away.

The rain arrived later than expected that day, but when it came, it was instantly heavy, as if somebody had suddenly turned on an overhead tap at full power. Olivia was looking out the living room window at the time, studying the charred remains of the Pontiac on the driveway. Bear had promised to remove the vehicle within a few days, but in the meantime, it would serve as a constant reminder of her night of terror. Yet even pondering the overnight attack didn't distract her from thinking about Cal. She'd thought about him constantly since he'd left the house three hours ago. They'd sat out in the yard together for an hour, reminiscing about their high school days, cracking up with laughter when remembering Cal's teasing behavior and pranks. She could see it all in a new light now. Cal had only ever wanted her attention.

The short interlude had served to chase away the lingering sense of danger. Cal managed to make her feel normal again. If only she could move past her sorrow at losing the café to him. The situation wasn't his fault, and he'd done everything to lessen her pain, but the issue remained a thorn in her side. Could she start a romantic journey with Cal while watching him take charge of Moretti's? Or would it prove too difficult?

"How are you holding up, Olivia?" her father asked, coming into the room.

"I'm okay." She gave him a reassuring smile. "I know you're worried, but this guy will be caught soon."

"And in the meantime, we're blessed to have Cal helping out," he said. "I saw you both having a cozy chat in the yard earlier. Is he becoming someone special?"

Her father had harbored hopes for a long time that Olivia would find a husband. He wished to see his daughter settled with a man who treated her with deep love and respect. And Cal was exactly the type of man he'd encouraged her to date.

"He is. And on top of that…he's offered me a business partnership at Moretti's," she said. "He knows I have no investment capital. I've turned him down, of course. The deal isn't fair to him. I'd feel like I was taking advantage of his good nature, and he'd wind up regretting it."

She had expected her father to be impressed with Cal's generosity. She thought he might even try to persuade her to change her mind. But far from being pleased, he instantly looked worried.

"Do you remember what I told you about the expensive running cost associated with Moretti's?" he said. "The one that can only be inherited by a member of the Moretti family?"

"Of course I remember," she replied.

He sat down in an armchair. He looked exhausted.

"If you go into partnership with Cal, the payment will become due once again."

"Because I'm a Moretti?"

He nodded. "I'm glad you rejected the deal. It was the right decision. After you were turned down for the business loan, I thought that would be the end of it. I hadn't anticipated Cal making such a kind offer."

Olivia sat on the couch, trying to approach this topic sensitively. She didn't want to fight with her father, but neither did she want to be fobbed off again. Whatever this situation was, it was clearly a Moretti family problem, and she felt she had the right to know.

"Tell me what's going on, Dad. Is this something to do with Sadie Billingham's murder? Was Nonno being blackmailed? He's been dead six years now, and Sadie's body has been uncovered, so there are no more secrets to keep." She tried to force him to look at her. "Right?"

But her father just shook his head, looking sad and guilty and generally wretched. "Wrong. Your grandfather made an admission to me on his deathbed, and I promised I'd never reveal it. That's why I can't be open and honest with you. It's imperative I keep my word."

Olivia felt her mouth drop open in shock. A deathbed confession? This was getting more curious by the day.

"Did he admit to killing Sadie?" she asked.

"No," her father replied. "He said…"

Leonardo stopped.

"Said what?" Olivia was hanging on his every word.

Her father stood up abruptly, as if suddenly coming to his senses. Olivia saw the metaphorical shutters come down over his eyes.

"I'm sorry, Olivia," he said. "I made a promise to your grandfather, and I can't break it. But please trust me when

I say it's not wise to accept Cal's offer. Let the café go, and let the past stay in the past."

He stood and walked from the room, while she stared after his departing figure. The complexity of this situation couldn't possibly get any worse.

Or could it?

Sitting at the kitchen table, Olivia flicked through an old photograph album her grandmother put together years before. She smiled at old family pictures, taken at home, on the beach and in the café. She'd always lived in a multi-generational household, with her parents and grandparents. This type of setup was commonplace in Italian culture, and Olivia felt she'd benefited from it. Although Mario had been a strict disciplinarian, he'd also brought positive habits to the household. He'd had an excellent work ethic and had given his all to the café, but at the same time, he hadn't let work take over his life. He'd believed strongly in long, leisurely dinners and had had a deep reverence for art and opera. Puccini had often blared through the kitchen when he made a batch of desserts on a Sunday.

On the other hand, there was no doubt that her grand-father had been a man of many faces, and some of them were unpleasant. Cal had been correct when he'd said family members were often complicated and messy. Cal was always right on the money lately. And his generous offer had proven to Olivia just how wonderful he was. He'd been prepared to hand over a 50 percent stake in Moretti's, with no guarantee of a return on his investment. She'd always appreciate that he'd made the offer, even if she couldn't accept it, especially after her talk with her father. The last thing she wanted to do was to saddle Cal with a running cost that would put him out of business. She just wished she knew what the cost referred to. Was it a gangster debt her grandfather had built up? Or an extortion payment? Whatever it was, she didn't think her father would tell her. But in the back of her mind, she wondered if it was related to the attacks she'd been subjected to.

Her cell began to buzz on the table next to the photograph album, and an unknown number lit up the display. She answered the call with a wary "Hello," uncertain of who might be on the other end of the line.

"Hello, Olivia?" It was a female voice. "It's Gina from the Hangout Bar."

"Oh." Olivia hadn't expected any follow-up from their conversation a few days ago. "Hi, Gina. How are you doing?"

"I'm good." Music played in the background alongside the occasional click of a pool ball hitting a cue. "I remembered something about the night Sadie vanished. It might be nothing, but since you seemed to want to know as much as you could, I thought I'd call anyway."

"I'm actually not investigating the details of the murder any longer," Olivia said. "But it's kind of you to call. Go ahead and tell me what you know."

"Well, I told you how I turned up for work the day after Sadie disappeared and found a letter saying she'd left for New York, but I forgot about the security tape. Back in those days, we had old-style security cameras that recorded onto tape. We used to let the cameras run through the night, inside and out, and in the morning, we'd review the footage to check there'd been no trouble overnight. Motorcycle gangs tried to break in sometimes. But on the morning I found Sadie's letter, the security tapes were gone. I didn't think much of it at the time, but now I'm wondering who took them."

"I'm sorry to say it was probably my grandfather who

stole them," Olivia said. "I think he must've killed Sadie in the bar and transported her body to the café to bury her in the cellar. Those tapes would've contained all the evidence to send him to prison, so he'd never have left them behind."

"Yeah," Gina said. "That's what I thought, but I figured I'd let you know."

"Thank you, Gina. I appreciate you thinking of me."

After hanging up the phone, Olivia placed it on the table and began to flick through the pages of the album again. Seeing herself as a young girl, flanked by her smiling mother and father, stirred a deep longing within her. She craved a family of her own with a husband who would cherish and protect her. That man might've been Cal if the circumstances hadn't conspired against them. But it might be a moot point anyway. Olivia had no idea of the depth of his feelings. He might not be looking for a wife. For all she knew, he wanted a casual relationship with no commitment.

Entering a partnership of any type with Cal seemed to be risky—and after all the danger she'd faced lately, she thought she might want to play it safe for a while. Once her attacker was caught, she might even consider moving to a neighboring town to look for work. Then she could avoid passing Moretti's each day and catching sight of the striped awning, gold lettering and cherry red door. The memories triggered by these things would hit hard.

She didn't know where she would end up, but she tried to accept her fate with grace. The end of an old life signaled the beginning of a new one. She was smart and resourceful enough to create a café of her own in the future, once she felt strong enough. It wouldn't be called Moretti's, but it would be hers and hers alone. She could start afresh.

Going solo seemed to be the best way forward.

* * *

Cal knocked on the door of the Moretti house early in the morning. He was wearing full waterproof clothing, having just visited the reservoir to catch up with the team from the Dam Bureau. They'd decided the dam was in serious danger of breaching, and they had asked the mayor to issue an evacuation notice for all residents living in the water's path. Cal's fire crew and Bear's deputies were currently knocking on doors at Redwood Estates, advising people to pack essential items only and make their way to Abbeywood Church. The rain was still falling and was forecast to continue for another twenty-four hours. It was the worst rainfall New Hampshire had experienced in living memory.

"Lord," he prayed quietly, waiting for the door to be answered. "Protect Your people from harm and comfort those in turmoil. They need You."

"Hi, Cal." Leonardo seemed surprised to see him. "I heard about the evacuation on the local news. Everything going okay down at Redwood Estates?"

"Yeah. We'll have everybody cleared out by this afternoon and hopefully they can go back home in two days." He raised his eyes skyward. "Providing the rain stops and the dam holds."

"You here to see Olivia?" He opened the door wide and invited him inside. "She's been quiet this morning. I think she's pining for you."

Cal stepped onto the mat, ensuring he didn't go any further due to his wet clothing.

"You think so?" He hoped this was true. "I can't stay long. I only have a few minutes."

"I'll go get her. She's sitting with her grandmother upstairs. My mother's feeling a little sick today, so we're keeping her warm in bed."

"Sorry to hear that, Leonardo. I'll wait here." Cal looked down at the mat. "I'm dripping like a wet dog, and I don't want to ruin your wood floor."

As Leonardo disappeared up the stairs, Cal practiced the words he'd been rehearsing all morning, muttering them under his breath while watching himself in the hallway mirror. He hadn't shaved for a few days, and his stubble was longer than he preferred. His sandy hair was also flat against his head after being shoved under a hood for too long. He wasn't looking his best, but he had no time to waste on sprucing himself up. Not when this impending conversation was so important. As soon as he'd decided to give free rein to the words on his heart, he knew it couldn't wait.

"Hi," Olivia said, coming down the stairs wearing blue jeans and a vivid red sweater. Her hair was tied up in a ponytail and it bounced on each step. "I thought you'd be busy this morning."

"I am," he said. "But I can snatch a few minutes to see you." He cast a gaze up and down her figure. "You look great."

She colored a little. "Thank you."

He took a deep breath and exhaled slowly.

"I couldn't sleep last night," he started. "I was thinking about all the things I didn't say to you yesterday."

"Like what?"

"Like I love you." He waited a few seconds before continuing. A declaration like that required time to sink in. "I think I've probably loved you since high school, but I never imagined there was a chance you'd feel the same way, so I wouldn't admit it, even to myself. But since we've gotten close recently, I haven't been able to deny it any longer. I keep catching myself imagining us building a future together, not just in Moretti's but in every part of our lives. I know you don't feel comfortable taking a business partnership, but it's being offered alongside my love and dedication to you. Who knows—maybe our journey will take us all the way to the altar." He paused for breath. "I want you to know the strength of my feelings before you walk away from Moretti's. Or walk away from me."

She stared at him, blinking fast, gripping onto the post at the bottom of the staircase. He waited patiently for her to speak, while water dripped silently from his waterproofs onto the mat beneath his feet. The silence was torturous.

"I love you too, Cal," she said at last, sending his belly flipping. "You're the most amazing and selfless man I've ever known. I wish I could take everything you're offering me and give you my devotion in return, but I can't. My father's hiding something sinister that's tied directly to our family. If I become your partner—in the café or in life— I'm afraid you'll get caught up in it."

He looked at her in confusion. What was she talking about?

"What do you mean?"

Olivia sat on the bottom step and told Cal about the mysterious deathbed confession her grandfather had made to his son. She told him about the unknown running cost that could only be inherited by a Moretti. And finally, she told him about her fears that Mario had been fraternizing with gangsters, perhaps even the Mafia. This seemed to be the only explanation for her father's secrecy.

"The Mafia?" Cal couldn't quite believe what he was hearing. "In sleepy Abbeywood?"

"I know it sounds crazy, but I can't think of any other reason why my dad would refuse to tell me. He's clearly paying somebody a lot of money each month, which is why Moretti's is heading for bankruptcy. It has to be related to the deathbed confession my grandfather made. It can't just be about Sadie—the truth of that's already out, but my dad has made it clear that the problem hasn't gone away. Nonno must've gotten caught up in something terrible, and Moretti's is paying the price for it. Literally."

Cal wanted to go to hold Olivia, to reassure her that everything would be fine, but he'd assured Leonardo he'd stay put.

"Do you think this is related to the attacks on you?" he asked.

"Maybe," she said. "I can't be sure of anything, because my dad won't discuss it. He says he made a promise to Nonno, and he won't break it." She covered her face with her hands. "Oh, Cal, I can't stop imagining the worst. Do you think my family is safe?"

He made the decision to go sit next to her on the step. He would apologize to Leonardo later for getting the floor wet.

"You and your family will be safe as long as I have a breath in my body," he said, taking her hand. "We'll get to the bottom of this, I swear."

"How?"

"I don't know, but I'll start by having a conversation with Leonardo. He's the key to uncovering this secret."

"I'm scared, Cal," she said, looking at him with her deep brown eyes. "I don't want anything bad to happen to you."

"It won't." He couldn't be sure of this, but Olivia needed to hear reassuring words. "As long as you love me, I think I might be invincible."

She smiled even as she shook her head. "You're not invincible, Cal. None of us are."

His radio crackled to life beneath his jacket, filling the space with the voice of an emergency dispatcher.

"Calling Abbeywood Fire Department. We've received

reports of an RTA on Route Four at the Franklin Crossroads. Two occupants of a vehicle are trapped. Please respond."

He lifted his jacket and unclipped the radio from his belt.

"This is Chief Caleb Mackenzie. I'll ask my team to head there immediately with cutting equipment, and I'm en route myself. ETA twelve to fifteen minutes." He stood up and looked down at Olivia. "I gotta go, but I'll be back as soon as I can."

She stood to face him, and he planted a kiss on her lips, before making his way to the door.

"Lock up behind me and don't go anywhere," he said. "Stay home. Stay safe. I love you."

He headed out the door, placing a radio call with his deputy to coordinate the response to the accident. It would deplete the manpower available at Redwood Estates, but it couldn't be helped.

Added to the stress of the day was Olivia's unexpected news. Cal planned on speaking to Olivia's father as soon as possible. The information Leonardo was withholding was an obstacle to Cal and Olivia's partnership, in every sense. Furthermore, it might provide a clue to the identity of her attacker. They couldn't start a life together until her stalker was caught.

Cal would walk barefoot through hot coals to be with Olivia. He would take whatever action needed to ensure they stood a chance of happiness.

TEN

Lying on her bed, staring at the ceiling, Olivia's mind gave her no rest. After Cal had left the house, she'd gone into the living room and sat next to her father to gently ask for more details about the payments he made each month. She'd mentioned her concerns regarding gangsters or the Mafia, and Leonardo had dismissed them out of hand, but he'd still refused to give her any answers. When she tried to press, he'd switched off the television and headed into the kitchen to prepare Francesca's afternoon snack. She'd then admitted defeat and trudged up to her room to curl up on her bed.

Beneath her sadness, another emotion fizzed inside— excitement. Cal loved her, and that piece of news sent her spirit soaring in spite of everything. He'd even referenced his hopes of marrying. The strength of his feeling gave her goose bumps all over. Their confirmed love for one another made everything seem possible, even a business partnership. But there was no way she could become a part owner of Moretti's while her father's secret threatened to derail the business.

"Worrying about it won't change anything," she said, pressing the heels of her hands into her eye sockets. "Everything will be okay."

"Penny?"

Olivia looked up to see her grandmother in the doorway, wearing her long white nightgown. She'd started calling Olivia by her mother's name more and more lately, her
mind retreating to the time when Olivia was a baby and her
parents were a young couple, in the first few years of their
marriage. Francesca inched her way into the room, looking around as if seeing it for the first time. Olivia jumped
from her bed.

"Let's get you back to bed, Nonna," she said, taking her
grandmother by the arm and leading her back into her own
room. "Dad is fixing you a snack. You need to keep your
strength up."

Her grandmother's skin was clammy and pale, and Olivia stroked her white hair after tucking her up in bed.

"Don't worry, Nonna," she said, sitting on the bed as
her grandmother began babbling in Italian again, making
repeated reference to Mario. "I'm here to take care of you.
I'm Olivia, your granddaughter."

Once again, the word *omicido* punctuated Francesca's
mutterings, except this time Sadie's name was used alongside it, as well as reference to a bar with neon signs. Olivia had been improving her rusty Italian with the use of
an app on her cell phone and she felt confident in her ability to understand her grandmother's ramblings. Francesca
was talking about the night of the murder and describing
the scene. But how could she know?

"Tell me what happened, Nonna," Olivia said, taking
her grandmother's papery hand. "What happened to Sadie
Billingham?"

"Olivia! Stop it!" Her father came into the room and put
down a plate of fruit on the dresser. "Your grandmother
should be resting."

Olivia stood up. "But she knows what happened on the night Sadie was killed. She's describing it to me. How could she know this stuff, Dad? Was she there?"

"No, she wasn't there." The color had drained from her father's face. "Your grandmother was at home, and she had nothing to do with it." He pointed a finger at her. "Do you hear me? She had nothing to do with it."

Leonardo's over-the-top reaction took her by surprise. She'd never seen him so angry and scared, and it took her a few moments to figure out why. She staggered backward as the truth hit her like a freight train. Her hand flew to her throat, and she let out a series of quick and ragged breaths, looking between her father and her grandmother.

"Nonna killed Sadie," she said when she was able to speak again. "And Nonno covered it up by burying the body in the cellar of the café. He was protecting her." The details came to her in stages. "And that's what he confessed to you on his deathbed, wasn't it?"

In the next moment, her father was shepherding her out of the door of her grandmother's bedroom. When the door was firmly closed behind them, he focused on her with wide and panicked eyes.

"Please, Olivia," he said. "Don't speak about this matter in front of your grandmother."

"So it's true?" she asked, still in disbelief. "Nonna *did* kill Sadie?"

"Yes, it's true." Her father let out a huge sigh, as if the weight of the awful secret had lifted from his shoulders. "I didn't know until six years ago, when your grandfather was dying. I made a vow to him that I'd never tell you, but I hadn't anticipated the problems dementia would bring. Your grandmother has talked of nothing else recently. She doesn't know what she's saying."

"Tell me what happened. I need to know."

Her father gripped onto the handrail on the landing, as if steadying himself.

"Your grandmother wasn't as clueless as people thought regarding your grandfather's affair. She had her suspicions for a long time. On that night, Sadie called your grandfather at the house, threatening to tell your grandmother about the affair. When he got in his car and drove to the Hangout Bar to have it out with her, your grandmother followed him in her own car. She confronted them both at the bar. Your grandfather confessed to the affair and promised to end it there and then. Sadie flew into a rage and attacked your grandmother. Your grandmother fought back. The Hangout Bar always had a small mascot figure next to the cash register. It's wrought iron, so it's heavy. Your grandmother picked it up and hit Sadie over the head, cracking her skull. She died instantly."

When visiting Gina, Olivia had noticed an iron sculpture of a motorcycle rider by the register on the bar.

"That's what killed Sadie?" she asked. "For thirty years, the murder weapon has been right there on the bar?" She shook her head, realizing it was the wrong choice of words. "But it's not murder, right? It was self-defense because Nonna had no choice."

"That's what your grandfather said, but he didn't call the police because he was terrified your grandmother would go to prison. Or worse. Back in those days, the death penalty was still in effect in New Hampshire. Even if she was acquitted, she'd likely still have to go through the humiliation of a trial, with her family's business aired out in all the newspapers. He made the decision to conceal the body and forge a letter from Sadie so he could pretend she had skipped town. I'm not saying it was the right decision, but he was trying to protect his wife."

Olivia shook her head, trying to make sense of this. It was a lot to take in.

"Did you tell Mom?" she asked.

"I told no one, not even your mother. I made a solemn promise to your grandfather that I'd protect your grandmother's reputation, no matter what."

"I can't believe it." Olivia looked at the rows of family photographs lined up on the wall. "All this time, Nonno and Nonna were the only people who knew what happened to Sadie."

"Not exactly." Leonardo rubbed his bald head where it was beginning to form beads of sweat. "This is where it gets complicated."

"What? You mean it gets more complicated than this?"

"Somebody else was at the bar. Somebody watched the murder take place."

"Who?"

"Randy Billingham. He went there to give Sadie a ride home, and he saw what happened through a window. After Sadie was killed, he went inside and offered to help your grandfather bury the body."

"Why would he do that?"

"Why do you think?" her father said scornfully. "For money. He blackmailed your grandfather by threatening to go to the police. Your grandmother's fingerprints were on the iron sculpture used to kill Sadie, and there was security footage of the incident."

"But it was self-defense," she argued. "Nonna was attacked first."

"Randy took the security tape. He said the camera angle didn't capture Sadie attacking your grandmother. It only showed the two women fighting as they moved close to the register and into the camera's view. There was no audio. Just the image of what happened in the last moments of Sadie's life. Who knows how a jury would have taken it? Your grandfather didn't want to take the risk. He paid Randy ten thousand dollars for his silence."

"But Randy wanted more, didn't he?" Olivia asked. "Ten thousand obviously wasn't enough."

"He started to treat your grandfather like a personal ATM, insisting on monthly payments. But they were affordable for a thriving business. When your grandfather was dying, I assured him I'd continue the payments to Randy. They were manageable back then, but a couple of years ago, he ramped up his demands. I tried to reason with him, but he was insistent. The café has been struggling to make ends meet ever since. I told him he's forced me to sell up, but he doesn't care. He knows he's living on borrowed time, because as soon as your grandmother is gone, I won't pay him another penny anyway. I'm only doing it for her."

"When Nonna passes, will you report Randy to the police?"

Her father shrugged with heavy and careworn shoulders. "I don't know. Maybe. I might be considered legally at fault, too. After all, I was paying him to cover up a crime."

"Don't you see, Dad?" Olivia said. "He must be responsible for the attacks on me. I was asking too many questions and he got scared."

Leonardo shook his head vehemently.

"No. I called Randy a while back to make sure he isn't the culprit, and he assured me he has nothing to do with these attacks."

"And you believed him?" she asked incredulously.

"Yes, I believed him. The time you were attacked on

your way back from Granton, I saw him at the gas station on the other side of town. He couldn't have been in two places at once. If I thought for one second Randy was out to hurt you, I'd have gone to Bear and told him everything."

Olivia began to pace the hallway, her temper rising at the thought of Randy blackmailing her family for thirty years, using the profits of the café to pay the mortgage on his fancy home.

"Nonna has advanced dementia," she said. "She'd be safe from prosecution now, right? We can expose Randy's crime immediately and get him arrested for extortion."

"Your grandfather's main concern was preventing your grandmother's good name being dragged through the mud," her father replied. "I told him I'd safeguard her reputation as long she's still alive." He pointed to her bedroom door with tears in his eyes. "And she *is* still alive, despite her dementia. She has times when she's fully aware of what's happening around her. I don't want those last lucid moments to be spoiled if the truth comes out and she has to live with the consequences. Even if she's not charged, everyone will still know what she did. The shame of it would break her heart."

"This is all Randy's fault." Olivia's temper was now blazing. "How dare he think he can get away with this." She started walking down the stairs. "He's grifted off the Moretti family for too long."

"Don't do anything stupid, Olivia," her father called. "Please stay here."

She lifted the keys to her father's Buick from the hook on the wall and sunk her feet into her sneakers by the door. After learning that Moretti's Café was being sold, she'd lashed out at Cal. He'd borne the brunt of her anger with patience and tolerance. All the while, the real culprit was right under her nose. Randy Billingham was responsible for the demise of Moretti's, and she intended to confront him with his misdeeds.

She would make sure he didn't get away with this for another day.

"Stay calm, Leonardo." Cal could barely make sense of the garbled words on the other end of the line. "Slow down and take a deep breath."

"Olivia's gone, Cal," came the reply. "She's gone to find Randy. I couldn't stop her."

"Why does she want to see Randy?"

"It's a long story, but she's in danger. From Randy, but also from the storm. What with the situation at the dam, she might get caught in a sudden flood. You know where Randy lives, right? Can you go there and make sure she's safe?"

Cal put down the sandbag he was holding and walked to shelter from the rain under a store doorway. After cutting two casualties from a wrecked vehicle, his crew was currently shoring up flood defenses for homes and stores next to the rising levels of the Abbeywood River.

"Randy lives smack-dab in the middle of the evacuation zone," he said. "The whole complex is deserted. Olivia shouldn't enter the area under any circumstances."

He heard a sigh of relief from Leonardo. "Oh thank goodness," he said. "That means Randy won't be home, right? And hopefully once she realizes that, she'll come straight back."

"Actually, Randy is likely to be home," Cal replied. "He and Bobby refused to leave when my crew asked them to. They think the dam breach warning is a hoax. The fire department can't force them to vacate. Randy was hitting the bottle hard when I went to speak with him." He reached into his jacket pocket to pull out the keys to his truck. "Are you sure that's where Olivia went?"

"I'm sure. She took my car. She's really angry, Cal. I don't have time to explain the details, but you know how hotheaded she can be. She doesn't have her cell phone with her, so she's totally isolated, especially if Randy and Bobby are the only ones in the area. Check on her. Please."

Cal heard Leonardo's voice break, and he wondered what could've happened to cause Olivia to rush out into the rain to confront Randy.

"I'll go find her, Leonardo," he said. "I'm leaving right now."

Pocketing his cell, he called out to his crew, letting them know he had urgent business to take care of. Then he jumped into his truck, started up the engine and set the wipers to the highest setting. The rain was relentlessly hammering everything in its path. As soon as he pulled onto the highway, he was going against the flow of traffic, as a long line of cars drove away from the evacuation area. The recent landslide had been cleared by workers, giving folks easy access to Abbeywood Church. The only people now in the danger zone were likely to be Randy, Bobby and Olivia.

Why hadn't Olivia called him before rushing off? She must've discovered something about Randy that'd triggered a strong reaction. His blood ran cold as he wondered if Randy was the man attacking her. He pressed the gas pedal to the floor, anxious to reach Redwood Estates in super-fast time.

His cell began to ring from its position clipped to his dash, and he swiped the screen to answer. It was Bear, and he sounded worried.

"Cal, we have a serious situation at the reservoir," the sheriff said. "The cracks in the dam are opening up wider, and water is starting to leak through. The guys from the Dam Bureau will be activating the emergency siren to signal an imminent breach."

"Oh no." Cal's stomach dropped. "Olivia is at Randy's house on Redwood Estates. I'm on my way there now. How long do we have until the dam bursts?"

"Fifteen or twenty minutes probably."

"Okay," he said, screeching to a halt outside the quiet fire station. "That might buy me enough time."

"Godspeed, Cal."

He hung up the phone and carefully backed into the parking lot of the station, where a boat trailer was stored for water rescues. After positioning the rear of his truck directly in front of it, he jumped out and hooked the trailer to his tow hitch. Then he continued his journey on the highway, flicking his eyes between the road ahead and the small motorboat in his rearview mirror. The drive to Redwood Estates would usually take ten minutes, but he might not have that much time to spare. Cal needed to be hyperalert to the signs of breach. He'd no doubt hear the thundering rush of water before seeing it, giving him time to stop the truck, hop into the boat and ride the wave as soon as it hit. His truck would be washed away but it didn't matter. A vehicle could be replaced. Olivia couldn't.

He prayed as he drove, lifting Olivia's name to the Lord. She meant more to him than anybody else in the world and losing her simply wasn't an option. He had to find her. The alternative didn't bear thinking about.

Cal traveled as fast as he dared while towing a boat, all the while keeping an ear turned to the open window, listening for the flood siren or the sound of a huge volume of water surging toward him. The road was deathly quiet, with nothing but the sound of rain on the roof of the truck.

He prayed that the woman he loved was currently safe and would be able to reach higher ground once the waters began to rise around her.

But in all probability, Cal was her only hope of survival.

Olivia turned the handle of Randy's front door and was surprised to find it unlocked. She had knocked on the door and rung the bell numerous times already, receiving no answer. The entire housing estate was like a ghost town due to the evacuation order. Yet Randy's truck was parked in the driveway, and she could see lights on inside. It appeared that Randy had remained behind, so she walked inside, intending to check. She didn't plan on staying longer than a few minutes—just long enough to speak her mind.

"Randy!" she called. "Are you home, you lying, cheating weasel?"

She heard a peal of laughter coming from the couch and walked across the rug to find Randy sprawled on the cushions with a glass of amber liquid in his hand. He was unmistakably drunk.

"I guess you know the truth at last," he said, still laughing. "Your dad finally told you, huh? I knew you'd react like a firecracker when you found out." He sipped his drink. "I like you, Olivia. You're headstrong like Sadie was."

"You stole from us," she said, pointing an accusatory finger. "You stole our livelihood."

"And your grandparents stole my wife!" he shouted, sitting up abruptly, sloshing alcohol onto his pants. "Your grandfather stole Sadie's heart, and your grandmother stole her life. I watched my wife die through a window, and I couldn't do anything to save her. Why shouldn't I be compensated for the pain they put me through?"

"But why push us to the point of bankruptcy? It makes no sense. It's not like it does you any good either."

"Your grandmother's not gettin' any younger, in case you hadn't noticed. As soon as the old lady is dead, I figured your dad would stop paying, so I had to make hay while the sun was shining."

"How dare you talk about her like that," Olivia said. "She's a person, not your collateral."

Randy glared at her. "She's a murderer."

"It was self-defense!" Olivia yelled. "Sadie attacked her first."

"I don't think a jury would've seen it that way. I could've put your grandmother behind bars for a long time with my testimony. The security footage didn't show how the fight started, only how it ended. You should be thanking me for saving her from the trial and the jail time she might have served. Instead, you've been making trouble and causing me problems."

A seed of worry planted itself in Olivia's belly. She had rushed to Randy's house in a fit of temper, but she was now uncomfortably aware that she was isolated and alone. She hadn't even brought her cell phone with her.

"You're the man behind the attacks, aren't you?" she asked, slowly backing away with small steps. "You're terrified of the truth coming out." She looked out the window, toward the garage. "I'm guessing you kept Sadie's old Pontiac out of sight all these years."

Randy put down his glass on the coffee table and let out a big sigh. Then he stood up and stuck his thumbs into the belt loops of his jeans, swaying on his feet.

"I only intended to scare you off your investigation. That's why I went to the café on the night you discovered Sadie's body. I wrote the message on the mirror and chased you into the cellar. Fighting with Cal Mackenzie in the water nearly killed me, and I realized I was being stupid. I'm too old to be running around like I'm twenty-five. I put a stop to it there and then."

"But you didn't," she said. "You continued your campaign against me."

"No, somebody else did." He rubbed a hand down his booze-reddened face. "When you paid me a visit the day after Sadie's body was discovered, you got me all worked up and I couldn't lie to Bobby any longer. I told him the whole story of how his stepmother died—and how I paid for this house with extortion money. I always told him our money came from a big lottery win thirty years ago, and he believed it. After he got over the shock of learning the truth, he was madder than a hornets' nest about the Morettis killing his stepmother. Then he got mad about you coming here and stirring the pot. He told me he was going to the garage to lift some weights and work off steam, but he must've taken the Pontiac and raced after you. I didn't even know he'd gone."

As the facts became clearer, Olivia felt her skin grow clammy with fear, and she continued to back away with tiny steps.

"Bobby must really hate me."

Randy nodded. "The person he blames most for all of this is Mario. He was the one who had an affair with Sadie and created a bad situation. But Bobby can't kill a man who's already dead, so you're the next best thing. The way you defended that awful man really got under his skin."

"I don't defend my grandfather anymore," she said. "I've realized how flawed he was, how he hurt people. He didn't kill Sadie, but he put her in an awful position."

"Doesn't matter." Randy shrugged nonchalantly. "Bobby

holds on to a grudge. He's looking to hurt a Moretti, and you're the one he's picked."

Olivia finally backed all the way to the door and reached behind to press the handle. But the door now seemed to be locked. She pressed the handle again and again, hoping it was simply stuck.

"You knew who was trying to hurt me," she said. "And you lied to my father when he asked you about it."

"No, no, no, I never lied. When Leonardo asked me if I was targeting you, I told him it wasn't me—which was the truth. I didn't have a clue what Bobby was doing until Cal mentioned the Pontiac Firebird. I kept that car in my garage ever since Sadie died. It was something to remember her by, and I never drove it. But Bobby was taking it out behind my back and using it to terrorize you. I was so angry when he burned it up on your driveway. I lost a little piece of Sadie when he did that."

Panic was setting in for Olivia. The door refused to budge. Someone had apparently locked it from the outside.

"So why didn't you stop him when you found out what he was doing?" she asked, hoping to keep him talking while she tried to figure out a way to escape. "You let him continue."

"I tried my best," he said, beginning to slur as the effects of his whiskey hit hard. "I even took away his guns. I told him Sadie wouldn't want him to become a killer, but he's too lost in grieving to listen to reason. For him, it's like Sadie only just died. For thirty years, he's wondered where she was and why she never called. He's determined to make somebody pay for the pain that your family put him through."

Olivia skirted around the wall, heading for the kitchen, where she hoped the door would be unlocked. She had to get out of the house as fast as possible. Randy stumbled across the rug toward her.

"Bobby's a ruthless man when he sets his mind to something," he said. "And as soon as I found out what he was up to, I knew that I couldn't stop him. He even recruited Dennis to keep tabs on you and report your whereabouts. Bobby thinks Dennis is being a good friend by helping him out. He has no idea Dennis is only trying to cover up his affair with Sadie. He thinks his wife would leave him if she found out, and you seemed intent on raking him over the coals. He's not a smart man, so he's not really thought it through. He's just terrified of losing his wife."

Olivia recalled seeing the grocery store truck pass her on the road. Dennis had obviously called Bobby and set her up for attack.

"Where is Bobby now?" she asked, stepping onto the tiled floor of the kitchen. "Is he home?"

Dennis laughed, throaty and phlegmy due to his cigarette habit.

"Wouldn't you like to know?" he taunted.

"Yes," she said. "I would."

"I persuaded Bobby to stay home with me instead of evacuating with the others." He watched her inch toward the kitchen door. "I told him the dam breach rumor is a hoax. When the dam breaks, we'll both drown here. We'll die together before you get the chance to ruin our lives by going to the police."

"You want your son to die?" Olivia asked, shocked.

"What kind of life would he have if we lived? We'd end up in jail for everything we've done. Or worse, we'd be free but totally on our own with no more money coming in. Neither of us have held a job in thirty years. What do we know about supporting ourselves? I figure that dying is a lot easier." He shrugged. "Of course, now you'll die too, because Bobby will never let you leave. You should never have come here. You signed your own death warrant."

She reached the door and turned the handle while her back was pressed against it. She breathed a sigh of relief. It was unlocked. Turning to flee, she came face-to-face with Bobby, who was standing on the step with a screwdriver in his hand.

"Hi," he said with a sinister smile on his face. "I was in the garage when I saw you arrive." He pushed her back inside and shut the door. "I'm sorry I wasn't here to greet you. You see, I've been working on an old car of Dad's because my last one got burned out." His smile grew wider. "The police were searching for it, and it got a little too hot to handle, if you know what I mean."

He waved the screwdriver in front of Olivia's face, while Randy looked on, not saying a word or lifting a finger to defend her. She ran into the living room, knowing there was no way out.

"Don't do this, Bobby," she said, looking between him and his father. "We need to leave here right away. The dam will probably break at any moment, and we'll all drown."

Bobby laughed, exchanging a glance with his father that told Olivia everything she needed to know. Bobby trusted his father implicitly.

"There's nothing wrong with the dam," he said, full of confidence. "That boyfriend of yours just wants us all out of here so the sheriff can enter our homes and search for clues that'll lead them to the man who's trying to kill you." He shook his head while clicking his tongue. "But me and Dad are wise to their plan."

"No," she said, holding up a hand. "Your father's lying to you. He's hoping you'll both drown here so you won't have to face charges for everything you've done."

Bobby looked sharply at his father, who smiled while picking up his glass from the table.

"She's lying, son," he said calmly. "The dam is fine. I'd never put you in harm's way. And neither of us are going to prison. We're safe in every way."

In the face of Randy's lies, Olivia cast a gaze around the room, searching for an escape route. The only option was the staircase. How could she have been so stupid to get herself trapped in Randy's home? Only her father knew of her location. She hoped he had called someone to come to her aid. Cal perhaps? But she couldn't guarantee a knight in shining armor would arrive. She'd have to save herself. She'd gotten herself into this situation and she'd have to get herself out of it.

"Don't bother trying to run," Bobby said, following her line of sight to the stairs. "There's nowhere to go, and any-ways…"

He stopped speaking, as a wailing sound cut through the air. The noise undulated between high and low pitch, re-minding Olivia of a wartime siren. It was a reservoir alert, warning the townsfolk of an imminent dam breach. Tak-ing advantage of Bobby's distraction, Olivia bolted for the stairs, taking them two at a time, jumping over piles of old magazines and stacks of junk. She kicked them behind her, hoping to slow Bobby's chase, but she could hear that he was hot on her heels. Flinging open the first door she saw, she entered a bedroom and slammed the door shut behind her, sliding a small bolt across the center. Then she tipped a heavy dresser onto its side, and it fell directly across the door, giving her some time to think. Bobby kicked the door from the other side, splintering the wood and cussing loudly when he wasn't able to bust it open right away.

Looking around the room, she saw nothing but piles of

clothes and a cluttered bed. She flung the pants and sweat-shirts aside, searching for a cell phone or electronic device. She found nothing of any use. She had to get out of there quickly, but the only viable exit was through the window. Opening it as wide as possible, she yanked the twin-size mattress from the bed and dragged it across the room. Lifting it up and squeezing it through the window proved almost impossible, but Olivia was spurred on by the knowledge that Bobby would soon succeed in gaining access to the room. After pushing the mattress out, she climbed onto the windowsill and swung one leg through. Then she focused her attention on the tatty mattress in the backyard below.

Preparing to jump, she heard a roar above the siren. It was the sound of gushing water and snapping trees. Then the flood came into sight as it poured down the highway, devouring everything in its path. In a few seconds, it had tossed the mattress aside and shattered the downstairs windows of the house. She heard Randy cry out, but the sound only lasted for a few moments. He must've become engulfed and swept away with the current. The noise of the water was deafening, thundering around her as if she was standing beneath a waterfall.

She felt Bobby's hand grip her arm and she tried to shake him free as he stepped onto the outside ledge. They both perched tenuously on the window frame, grappling with one another. As she jerked her arm away, they both lost their footing—though she and Bobby somehow managed to cling onto the plastic frame. They dangled above the treacherous water by their fingertips.

"This is where it ends, Olivia," Bobby shouted. "This is where you die."

"You're going to die, too," she replied.

"I'm counting on it," he said, with a smile. "I'm gonna go be with my dad."

With that, he let go of the ledge and disappeared beneath the bubbling brown water below.

Cal pushed the boat to full throttle, bouncing over the waves of the flood. He could see the roofs of Redwood Estates above the tree line, but he couldn't tell if he was traveling over the highway or fields. By now, everything beneath him was covered with murky water, filled with uprooted trees. His truck had floated past him, carried by the downward trajectory of the surging water. If Olivia had managed to make it to the second floor of a house, she stood a good chance of staying out of danger until he arrived.

But when he reached the housing complex, everything looked different. Which house was Randy's? Cal's bearings were all out of whack. Moving between the rows of roofs, he yelled at the top of his lungs, before stopping to listen.

He heard a faint response and did a U-turn, heading toward it. When he finally spotted Olivia's vivid red sweater, he was horrified. She was dangling above the water, clinging to the ledge of a second-floor window. Navigating as close as possible, he tied the boat's rope to the house's drainpipe to keep it steady.

"Jump, Olivia," he called, standing up. "I promise to catch you."

"I'm scared, Cal," she called back. "What if I go into the water?"

"Trust me. Just let go."

She obeyed his request and fell with a yelp of fear. He caught her squarely in his arms, before falling backward into the boat with their limbs tangled. With the boat securely tied to the pipe, he allowed her to lie there for a moment or two. He heard her giving thanks for her rescue and he joined in, uttering some thanks of his own.

"We have to stop meeting like this," he said, as she lifted her head to look into his eyes.

"How about meeting someplace else next time? Like on a date?"

"Sounds great," he said with a beaming smile. "Where do you want to go?"

"I know a really great café on Main Street," she said. "It's kinda flooded right now, but I've heard it's reopening soon under new management. The pastry chef makes the perfect panettone."

"The pastry chef is also beautiful from what I've heard."

Olivia cupped his chin and traced the outline of his lips with her thumb.

"She's off the market. She's in love with her business partner."

"And he's in love with her too. I think they'll be happy together."

"I agree."

Cal looked up at the house. "What happened here? Is anybody else inside?"

She shook her head. "They were, but it's just me now. Can you take me home? I'll explain everything once we get there."

"Sure."

He untied the boat, put one hand on the motor lever and the other in Olivia's. As she squeezed his fingers tight, they powered against the current under a dark and stormy sky. But in Cal's mind, it was the most beautiful sunset he'd ever seen.

EPILOGUE

The Mayor of Concord cut the ribbon across the door to a huge round of applause.

"It is a great privilege to open this wonderful facility on behalf of Cal and Olivia Mackenzie," the mayor said. "Sadie's Place will provide shelter to the city's homeless and vulnerable population. I wish the Mackenzies the best of luck in this charitable venture. Thank you for investing in our community."

Another round of applause resounded as everybody filed into the building, where a colorful cafeteria shared the open plan space with a seating area. Down the hallway was a prayer room, library, computer hub and beauty parlor. And the building next door was a dormitory, with beds for over a hundred people. The project had been a labor of love for Cal and Olivia, and the grand opening filled them both with a sense of enormous pride.

"This is great, huh?" Cal said, drawing Olivia into a hug. "I can't believe we finally did it."

"It's amazing, Cal," she said. "I'm glad we chose the name Sadie's Place. It's good to honor her life like this. I feel like I've righted a wrong somehow."

Surrounding Cal and Olivia were all the people who'd supported them during the last two years and who had helped raise much-needed funds to assist in setting up this facility. Rosalie and her husband, Martin, stood next to Olivia, passing a baby between them. Rosalie had given birth six months ago to a beautiful baby girl whom she'd named Lucy. She was currently on extended maternity leave from her job at the café but planned on returning soon, just in time for Olivia to take some leave of her own. Leonardo stood next to Cal's parents, Susan and Roger, admiring the murals on the walls and chatting amiably. In the foyer, Bear was showing Gina where Sadie's photograph hung on the wall, and Gina dabbed at her eyes even as she smiled. Meanwhile, Pastor Brian waved and smiled at Olivia and Cal, before making his way to the prayer room. The first thing he wanted to do was pray a blessing over the building.

It was important to Olivia that this facility would serve those residents of Concord whose lives might possibly mirror Sadie's. Many of those who'd already signed up to receive help had a history of family dysfunction, emotional abuse and alcohol or drug addiction. If Sadie had been able to access services like this, she could've possibly turned her life around and avoided seeking comfort in the arms of unkind men like Randy. Or married men like Mario. Sadie's Place offered more than beds and food. It offered counselling services, basic medical treatment and educational training.

"I'm glad your dad is here," Cal said, looking over at Leonardo, who waved enthusiastically. "He gets to see the legacy of Moretti's Café."

Olivia smiled at her father, wishing her grandmother was also there to see this momentous occasion. But Francesca had died peacefully one month after the Moretti's purchase contract was signed, officially making Cal and Olivia the café's new owners. They'd married in a small ceremony officiated by Pastor Brian six months later. They hadn't taken a honeymoon of course, because they were too busy expanding the Moretti's brand into the capital. Now there were three Moretti's Cafés in existence—the original in Abbeywood, plus two new ones in Concord. And all three were turning superb profits. Fifty percent of those profits had been funneled into the creation of Sadie's Place, alongside private donations and corporate sponsorship.

The facts about Sadie's death had spread like wildfire in Abbeywood when the truth came out, as Olivia knew they would. But she didn't mind. By that point, Francesca's condition had worsened to the point where she didn't hear a word of it.

"I'm gonna make a speech," Cal said, stepping onto a small stage that had been erected in the cafeteria. "I have a few things to say."

"Keep it clean," she joked.

Olivia sat on a chair, assisted by Rosalie, rubbing her belly over her loose-fitting dress. Her baby bump had become very large lately, and she'd been slowing down these last few days as her energy levels dipped. The pregnancy was the icing on the cake after all the other blessings she and Cal had received. Yet it hadn't been an easy journey. She'd been required to testify at the trial of Dennis Clark for aiding and abetting Bobby's campaign of terror against her. Dennis was now coming to the end of his two-year prison sentence and was expected not to return to Abbeywood. His worst fear had been realized, and his wife had initiated divorce proceedings. Randy's and Bobby's bodies were recovered from the water six weeks after they disappeared beneath the flood. They had paid the ultimate price for their misdeeds.

"Ladies and gentlemen," Cal began, standing in front of

the microphone. "Thank you for attending the grand open-ing of Sadie's Place here in Concord. My wife and I are overjoyed you could be here with us on this special day."

Olivia's skin tingled with happiness. Hearing Cal de-scribe her as his wife always gave her goose bumps.

"For many years, Olivia and I treated each other like en-emies," he continued. "We had the kind of fights usually associated with schoolyards." He held up his hands. "I was always the instigator."

He paused for the laughter that ensued, and Olivia smiled at him. She remembered those times only too well, but they were firmly behind them.

"We are living proof of the power of God," he said. "When we reconciled our differences and forgave every-thing in the past, we fell in love. God can heal any division and soothe any pain, as long as you let Him work in you. That's why we created Sadie's Place. This facility will be available to anybody who wants to escape a life of sadness and tragedy and become a new person. I'm so thankful for all the blessings I've received in my life, and I'm overjoyed to have the chance to share them with others." He gestured toward Olivia. "The biggest blessing in my life is my beau-tiful wife, Olivia, who you probably noticed is carrying our first child, a baby boy."

There was a ripple of applause, and Olivia stood up to acknowledge everybody's good wishes.

"Did you choose a name yet?" a voice called from the throng.

"We did," Olivia called back. "His name is Matteo. It means gift from God."

"And it's a great Italian name too," Cal said over the mi-crophone. "My family originally hails from Scotland, and my choice of Scottish name was firmly rejected."

Olivia cupped a hand at the side of her mouth to project her voice.

"He's not gonna be named Angus, Cal. Accept it already."

Cal shrugged nonchalantly, playing comically to the audience. Wearing a well-tailored dark suit and red tie, he was more handsome than she'd ever seen him. He may have hung up his fire chief's uniform for good, but he'd lost none of his protective instincts. His dedication to serving others remained strong, and Olivia couldn't have been prouder of him.

"I'd like to make a toast," Cal said, as waiters handed out glasses of sparkling apple juice. "To the woman who gave this shelter its name. Just like all of us here, she wasn't perfect, but her life mattered. We hope to bring peace to those who are hurting and show people their true value." He raised his glass high. "To Sadie."

"To Sadie," Olivia chimed in.

Cal winked at her from the stage, and she beamed at him for articulating the words in her heart. The tragic events of the past were beyond her control, but she could steer her future in a spirit of forgiveness and kindness. With Cal by her side, she knew anything was possible.

* * * * *

Dear Reader,

Cal and Olivia's story is a classic trope, in which rivalry turns into romance. Having been taught to dislike each other from childhood, their growing attraction generates all kinds of tension. Mario's dark influence in their lives created division, but God's hand unites them. Even Christians are not immune from feuds and friction, but if we submit to God, He will heal the wounds.

Francesca and Leonardo's characters were written from personal experience. Just like Leonardo, I am a caregiver for my mother, who was diagnosed with dementia a few months ago. This is a situation some of you will be experiencing in your own lives, as you care for loved ones. Memory loss can be cruel, but I have found great moments of joy in caring for my mother. She forgets me on occasion, but she somehow always knows we have a special bond. Love is a memory that is never lost, even when names, faces and events have faded from mind. Scripture assures us that nothing can separate us from the love of God. This is a source of great comfort for those suffering dementia and their caregivers.

Thank you for joining me on Cal and Olivia's journey. I hope to welcome you as a reader for my next story.

Blessings,
Elisabeth